super

ACTING

John Farndon

Illustrated by Jennifer Graham

Consultant:
Suzy Graham-Adriani,
Royal National Theatre

Hodder Children's Books
a division of Hodder Headline

Published by Hodder Children's Books 2000
Cover photograph by Simon Annand

Designed by Fiona Webb
Series designed by Fiona Webb

10 9 8 7 6 5 4 3 2 1

A catalogue record for this book is available from the British Library.

ISBN: 0340 77329 4

Printed by Clays Ltd, St Ives plc

Hodder Children's Books
a division of Hodder Headline
338 Euston Road
London NW1 3BH

Meet the author

John Farndon lives in London and has written lots of books for children, including the *Pocket Encyclopedia* (Dorling Kindersley) and the *Children's Encyclopedia* (HarperCollins). One of his specialities is making science fun and easy to understand, and he has twice been short-listed for the Copus Science Book Prize, with *How the Earth Works* and *What Happens When?* His real passion, though, is the theatre. He has acted in and directed all kinds of plays in London, Edinburgh and other places, and jointly runs a small theatre company. He has also written translations of the plays of Lope de Vega (*Dog in a Manger* and *Mad for Love*) and many original plays, including *The Naked Guest* and *Numismata.*

Introduction

Almost everyone, it seems, wants to act. And it's no wonder. In what other activity do you get to be a hero, or a villain, or a saint, or a clown, shout and scream, jump up and down, and do all kinds of other strange, outrageous things – and then get adults clapping you for it! Talk out loud to yourself anywhere else and people might call a psychiatrist to get you locked up. But if you're acting as Hamlet in Shakespeare's* play, you can call it a 'soliloquy', and people will say, "You were wonderful, darling!". Kiss the most gorgeous person in school and you'll probably get a slap in the face. But if you're acting in Shakespeare's *Romeo and Juliet*, you might get to kiss them again and again – and people will still say, "You were wonderful, daaarling!!" In fact, you can get away with murder as an actor.

The best thing about acting, though, is that it's FUN. Of course, it can be nerve-racking, but when you get it right it's a tremendous thrill. Serious actors will tell you the buzz they get from a good performance is better than the best roller coaster ride (and much more dangerous).

Whatever your reason for getting into acting, this book tries to provide a little guidance. It won't help you become Leonardo di Caprio or Kate Winslet (anyway, that's been done). But it may help you get the most out of acting, and avoid making a complete fool of yourself. (Unless, of course, you are trying to make a complete fool of yourself...)

* See the '*Want to know more?*' section at the back of the book.

Contents

1 What is acting?

Everyone's an actor in a way – you, your Mum and Dad, your friends, your teacher, the Prime Minister… The point is, all of us act differently in different situations. Without even thinking about it, you put on a different act with different people. You might play the joker with your best friends. Or the smooth-talker with some boy or girl you're trying to impress. Or the hard-working student at school (even though you're really a complete slacker).

Sometimes this is so subtle you're not aware you're doing it. Sometimes you know all about it and it's about as subtle as an Elephant in a Ballet Class – like you acting innocent when the last piece of cake mysteriously vanishes.

But this is not REAL acting, you might say. Not like on stage or on TV. Actually it is. The problem is that it's really hard to act to order. As soon as they have to think about what they're acting, most people become self-conscious and awkward. Try doing something as simple as taking a drink while thinking about every single movement – deliberately moving your fingers to grasp the glass and so on – and it all gets a bit like a jerky slow-motion replay. Acting naturally is the hardest kind of acting of all.

What makes acting on stage or TV or film different from everyday acting is that you're pretending to be someone (or some character) to tell a story and bring it to life. We'll come back to this shortly.

Kinds of acting

Of course, there is not just one way of acting, but dozens. Each is suited to a particular kind of performance, and each has its own skills and techniques.

- **Stage acting** means acting live in a theatre in front of an audience. People have been doing this at least since the days of Ancient Greece. There are all kinds of elaborate theories about acting for the stage, but for most actors now the aim is actually quite simple: to make it all like life only bigger. (It has to be bigger to be seen and heard at the back of the theatre.) Because the show is live, there is no chance to correct any mistakes, so for a professional stage play the actors rehearse for three to six weeks beforehand. Rehearsal also gives the actors a chance to develop their roles.

Laugh? I could have died

Actors sometimes talk about 'dying' on stage when they give a bad performance. But for the very earliest actors we know about, dying on stage was for real. The Abydos passion play was performed for the pharaohs of Ancient Egypt 5000 years ago. The play was about how the god Osiris gets ripped to pieces by his brother Seth, and then is restored to life by his wife Isis and son Horus. But the performances were so realistic they often needed a new actor to play Osiris in the second half...

- **TV and film acting** is quite different from stage acting. Although the aim is also to make the acting lifelike, the approach is in some ways just the opposite. Because the camera moves in so close, even a little gesture like raising an eyebrow looks gigantic, and nodding vigorously can make the actor's head bob in and out of the picture like a demented yoyo. So with TV and film acting, the aim is to make it like life, only smaller. In fact, the camera and the director do much of the work. This means there is not the same need to have long rehearsal periods to develop the role. There is more about this in Chapter 12.

Then there are various traditional approaches, which you only need to know about if you're interested – or want to drop into the conversation to impress people:

- **Mime** is one of the oldest kinds of acting and dates back at least to Roman times. It is basically silent acting, using gestures and movements but no words. The modern style of mime developed in France and one of the most famous mime artists is the Frenchman, Marcel Marceau (born 1923).
- **Noh and Kabuki** are Japanese traditional styles of theatre. In Noh, the actors wear very elaborate masks signifying a wicked man, a gracious lady and so on, and do everything in an exaggerated, stylized way. In Kabuki, they wear mask-like make-up. The actors are always male and usually specialize in one kind of role which they learn from their fathers and play all their lives.
- **Commedia dell'arte** (pronounced kom-ed-ear dell art-eh) is the boisterous style of the acting companies that started touring Italy in the 16th century, and became popular all over Europe. The same comic characters, like Harlequin the clown and Pantaloon the old man, appeared in every show, and the plots were all pretty similar too. So the actors had to be very funny and inventive (or just plain rude) to keep people interested.

Actors and luvvies

If you spend enough time with actors, you're bound to come across a luvvie or two! There are various kinds to look out for.

- *First of all there are the Kissers. Kissers are the ones who throw their arms around you and kiss you extravagantly, then while telling you how Marvellous you are let you know who is really marvellous (it isn't you).*
- *Then there are the Shiners – the ones who shine so brightly that everyone else is put in the shade – or so they think.*

- *And of course there are all the Bees Knees – the Queenbees (who don't care what the show is like as long as all you drones buzz round them), the Wannabees (who will be the The Next Big Thing, even if they have to kill to get there) and the Networkerbees (who know everyone who is anyone, or soon will do).*

All of these will do their best to put an end to your acting career. Don't let them!

Why me?

Why you indeed? The answer is because you want to. People often get put off acting because they believe they have no talent for it. But if you ask them just what a talent for acting is, they'd be hard pushed to say. Whatever talent is, it's not up to you whether you have it or not. What is up to you is whether you want to find out if you can do it – and whether you are willing to work on developing the skills you need to do it well. If your voice is quiet, for instance, or you have a habit of banging into tables when people are staring at you, it doesn't mean you can't act; it just means you have to work on making your voice louder and looking where you're going.

As an actor, you have to learn to look at yourself as honestly as you possibly can. Every now and then, you should make a list of your strengths and weaknesses, and then work steadily at overcoming your weaknesses and making the most of your strengths.

You do have to be brave. You're going to make a total prat of yourself every now and then. Nearly every actor has a tale or two of times when they just wanted to drop through the floor from embarrassment…

Make believe

There are two things an actor has to do. The first is to create an imaginary world convincingly.

When you were younger, you probably played games of make-believe. You might have played at being a doctor or an alien. You might have imagined you were fighting prehistoric monsters, or maybe you talked to a favourite teddy as if it were really alive. Sometimes you threw yourself into these games of make-believe so well that it was hard to be sure they were not entirely real.

As we grow older, we play these games less and less – or at least keep them to ourselves, and call them daydreams. It's OK to rush around making car engine noises and holding your hands on a pretend steering wheel when you're six. People start to think you're a bit odd if you're still doing it when you're eleven, which is a shame really, because it's great fun. And that's where acting comes in. Acting is all about creating imaginary worlds so convincingly that they seem real – not only to you, but to everyone watching, including other actors. So, many of the exercises later in this book are to help you get back what you did very easily when you were younger. There is a difference though. As an actor, unlike when you were young, you always have to be in control of your imagination, not simply let it run riot.

Telling a story

The second thing the actor has to do is tell a story, and this is something actors often forget. It's no good losing yourself in the role so completely that you forget about everything else, like you might in a game of make believe. The whole point is for you and the other actors to work together to tell the story to those watching. (Notice that bit about you and the other actors. It isn't about what you do alone; it's all about teamwork.)

Once upon a time...

A useful exercise when you're starting to act is to try telling a story to a small group – either younger children or other actors you know. Don't try to act out or perform the story at all. Just concentrate on getting the story across as simply and effectively as possible. Make sure that your listeners follow the story all the time and understand exactly what is going on. To be sure, ask them questions about it afterwards. If you can't think of a story, tell them the one about the Mouse That Ate New York, or the one about the First Girl on Mars. You don't know them? Well you'll have to make them up...

2 Groundwork

To be any good, an actor has to work on essential skills as well as being in plays. Just as a footballer has to practise ball skills in training and a pianist has to play scales, so an actor has to practise the basics before getting on to the real thing. The good thing is that many of these exercises are almost as much fun as acting in a play – especially if you do them with other actors.

As an actor, you don't have to master control of a racquet like a tennis player or a violin like a violinist. Your instruments are your body and your mind, and you have to practise to make them work together in the right way. Some exercises are geared more towards physical skills, like the exercises for your voice. But many speaking problems are not physical but in the mind, so even here the idea is to make the body and mind work in combination.

Hunks and wimps

There are those who say you have to be good-looking to hit the big time as an actor, and of course, it does help – if you can't act. For anyone who can act, looks are not an obstacle, and looks are actually what you make of them. Robert de Niro is still one of the world's biggest stars, yet he was so scrawny and pale when he was a kid growing up in New York that other kids taunted him and called him 'Bobby Milk'. No wonder, then, that his first acting role, at the age of ten, was The Cowardly Lion in The Wizard of Oz. Robert de Niro made the most of his nervousness in that role, and made so much of it in later life that he is famous for tense, tough roles – such as the head gangster, Vita Corleone in The Godfather II and the boxer, Jake la Motta in Raging Bull. The secret is not to be ashamed of the qualities you have that make you different, but to make the most of them. Now there are thousands of Robert de Niro imitators, but he was the first de Niro – and you could be the first YOU. There are roles for all kinds.

Getting warmer

Every sportsman and dancer warms up before beginning training to avoid straining muscles. An actor needs to warm up too. But for an actor, the warm-up has an additional purpose: it puts you in the right frame of mind. Without a warm-up, your thoughts are scattered all over the place and too buzzing with the events of the day to concentrate fully on acting. The warm-up helps calm you down and focus your thoughts.

Actors eventually develop their own warm-up routine, but here's one to get you going. The idea is to go through warming up every bit of your body. Of course, it's hard to do all this while reading so, if you can, get someone to read out instructions. If you can't, just go through section by section, memorizing the exercises before you do them.

WARNING

Make sure the place where you are exercising is safe: watch out for sharp corners! If you feel dizzy, stop and rest.

Energy release

Before you do anything else, get yourself completely worn out with a burst of something energetic:

1 Do ten star jumps really quickly. Fling your arms and legs out sideways as far as you can while jumping in the air.
2 Now run on the spot as fast as you can for one minute, then run around the room (without bumping into anything).

Warming up your legs

1 Stand on one leg. Lift the other leg and with your foot trace out a circle in the air while keeping the leg still – moving only at the ankle. Now bend your foot back into line with your leg – like a ballet dancer. Now stand on the other foot and repeat.
2 Sit on the floor with your legs spread out in a V, stretch out and touch first the toes on one foot, then the other.
3 Stand up and take a giant step forward with one foot. (Don't move the other foot.) Keeping both feet firmly on the ground, push both hands down on the front knee and bend it down as far as you can while staying balanced. Repeat for the other leg.

4 Find a wall it is OK to put your feet on. Now lift your leg and put one foot up on the wall at waist height. Touch the toes. Repeat with the other leg.
5 Finish off by standing on one leg and swing the other backwards and forwards as loosely as possible eight times. Repeat for the other leg.

Warming up your arms and shoulders

1 Stand up straight and stretch each arm up towards the ceiling in turn. This is a bit like climbing a ladder – except that you really have to stretch to reach each rung. The ladder has eight rungs.

2 Now stretch up your right arm and bend over sideways at the waist to the left as if you were trying to touch the far wall with your outstretched arm. Repeat with your left arm, bending to the right.

3 Hunch up your shoulders to your ears as if you were trying to hide your head. Then suddenly let them drop loosely.

4 With your right shoulder, make as big a circle in the air as you can – all the way round forward and all the way back. Do this four times. Now do the same for the left shoulder.

5 Shake out your arms as loosely and vigorously as possible – as if you were trying to shake some horrible sticky goo from your fingers.

6 Stretch out your arms as far as you can in front, with both hands clasped together. Do the same behind you.

7 Finish off by whirling your arms like windmills.

Warming up your neck and spine

1 Circle your head eight times in each direction.
2 Let your jaw hang open and your head fall gently back as far as it will go without effort. Now lower your chin on to your chest. Repeat four times.
3 Bend down at the waist till you're almost touching your toes – don't worry if you can't: just go as far as you can without effort. Now let your head, arms and upper body hang down as loose as you can. Let it flop around a few times like a rag doll.
4 Now gradually uncurl back up again, leaving your head till last. Try and pull up just a bit of your back at a time, uncurling it gradually, until you're left with just your head hanging forward. Then pull that up gently.
5 Repeat 3 and 4 four times.

Warming up your face

1 Stretch out your face as far as you can, opening your mouth wide and raising your eyebrows.
2 Scrunch up your face as small as you can.
3 Finish off by yawning several times – but don't go to sleep just yet!

Are you speaking or shouting?

Unless you want to be a mime artist, you need to know how to use your voice well. You have to be heard loud and clear throughout the theatre – even when you seem to be whispering. The audience would hear you if you shouted, but shouting would sound horrible and unnatural, and it would put your voice under tremendous strain. Since you may have to keep up your voice throughout a long play – not just once but night after night – you need to make yourself heard without strain. This is sometimes called 'projection'.

- **Breath power** What makes the sound of your voice is air from your lungs vibrating over the 'vocal cords' in your throat as you breathe out. When you shout, your voice is loud because the vocal cords are vibrating really hard – which is why shouting sounds harsh. But the vocal cords soon get overstretched by all this hard work and go slack, leaving you croaking like a frog. The secret to projection is to boost the sound by making your lungs do all the work instead. If you're breathing out more air you produce more sound while the vocal cords go on working in the same gentle way they do when you're speaking normally. This is why many of the voice exercises on the following pages are designed to control your breathing.

- **Keeping cool** Actually, most of us could speak louder quite well if we weren't nervous. Being nervous makes us tense, and tense muscles in the neck restrict the flow of air when you breathe – making your vocal cords work harder and putting your voice under strain. It's one of those really annoying little twists of life that when you get up in front of everyone to speak – the one time when you really want to speak with a beautiful, loud voice – you get all nervous and the tension makes you sound quiet and squeaky. This is why many voice exercises are designed to help keep you relaxed.

- **Wagging your tongue** Even with the biggest lungs in the world, you'll make no more sense than a gorilla unless you can make the right sounds. This is where tongue and lip exercises come in. If you hear actors reciting all kinds of strange and tricky phrases, this is why.

Soundbites

If you're in a group, why not try this game to help you develop the way you imagine and listen to sounds? Split the group in half. Half sit down with their eyes firmly shut. The other half decide secretly on a very simple, short scene or story they are going to create. The idea is to create it entirely with sounds they make with their voices – but not words – and their hands. Those with their eyes shut must listen and afterwards say what was going on. The aim is not to fool the listeners but to make sure they understand fully what is going on. The challenge is to paint a really complete picture in sound. You could try scenes such as these:

- **What I Did This Morning:** sleeping, waking up, getting dressed, going to the bathroom, having breakfast and so on. How might you convey each of these with a sound?

- **Out on a Date...**

Getting relaxed

1 Start by pretending to be a cool cat after a night on the tiles. Stretch and yawn, then get down on all fours and slowly arch up your back bit by bit. As you arch up take a deep breath in, and use the breath to help you. Now bow your back down as you breathe out. Repeat this four times.

2 Lie flat on the floor on your back with a small book under your head, and hands by your sides, palms up. Now work your way up your body, tensing then relaxing each set of muscles. Start by curling up your toes then relaxing them. Then clench and release all of the parts of your body shown in the diagram in turn (*toes, feet, calves, thighs, buttocks, chest, hands, arms, shoulders* and *neck)*. Finish with your face.

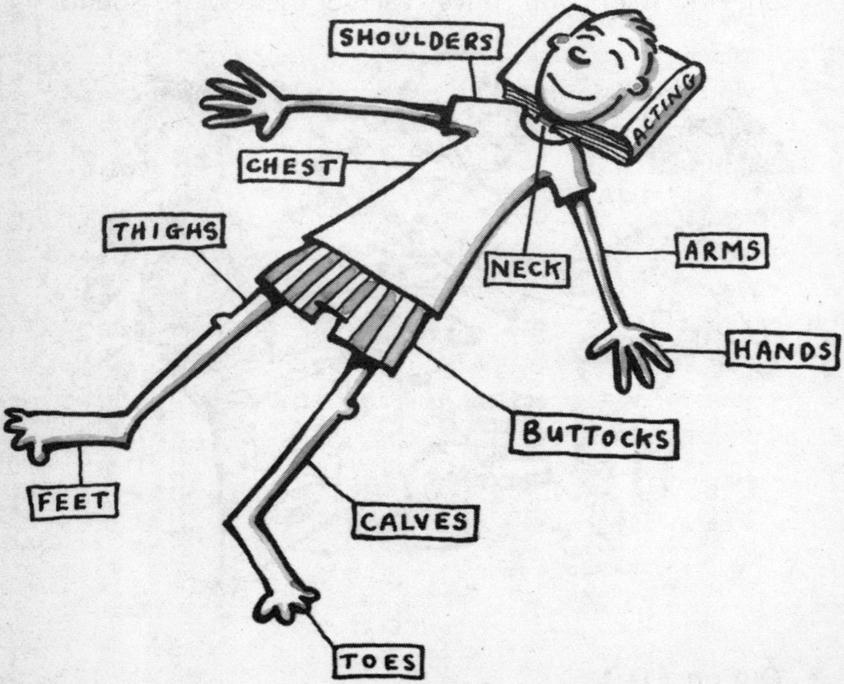

Bigger breaths

3 Now to build up your lung power, try to fill your lungs as deep you can. Put one hand flat on your chest and breathe in and out slowly, trying to gently push your hand up as the air fills your lungs with each in-breath. Now put the other hand lower down, just below your ribs (this is on the diaphragm) and try to raise this hand as you breathe in too. Each time you breathe in, try to push your hand out a little further, without straining. Each time you breathe out try to let your hands down slowly and in as much control as possible. IF YOU FEEL AT ALL DIZZY, STOP and wait before trying again.

4 Now you need to make sure your throat and mouth are as relaxed and open as possible so that the flow of air is not restricted. First yawn, then roll your head slowly from side to side with your jaw hanging open loosely. Now look at the ceiling directly above your head. Repeat step 3 breathing in through your nose and saying "Herrrr" as you breathe out through your mouth.

Breath control

5 To start improving your breath control, draw in a long, deep breath. Then breathe out in as slow and controlled a way as you can, saying "Aaaah" just as you would at the dentist's. Repeat this eight times, each time trying to breathe out more evenly so that the sound fades smoothly. Repeat twice more, trying to keep the sound level the same throughout.

Lion or mouse?

When most people start breath control exercises, they let a big rush of air out at the start of each out-breath, then struggle to keep a weedy stream of air going. If you do this you will start speaking like a lion on each breath and end up with a mouse-like squeak. The idea is to let your breath out as evenly as possible. To be sure this is what you are doing try one of these tests.

- *Light a candle, then take a deep breath and breathe out across the candle flame from close up – so slowly and gently that it bends over, but barely flickers, and stays alight.*
- *Hold a thin sheet of paper in front of your mouth. As you breathe out, blow on the paper and lift it slightly. Try to keep it lifted at the same angle throughout the breath.*

Tongue strengthening

1 Stand straight up with your feet slightly apart and look straight ahead. Relax.
2 Blow out your lips like an irritated horse.
3 Now chew as if the horse has been given some straw mixed with sticky toffee by some cheeky stable girl.
4 Poke out your tongue like the horse might at the stable girl.
5 Now push your tongue firmly first against your lower teeth, then your upper teeth.

Better letters

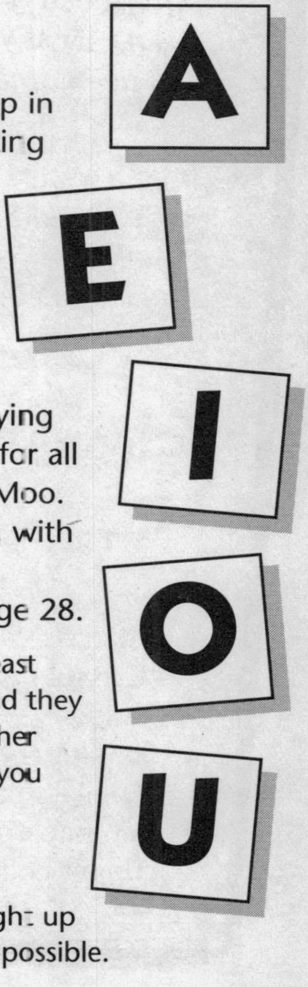

1 Say “Gar-oong”with the “Gar” bit deep in your throat and the”oong” bit resonating like a gong.
2 Start an out-breath by humming “mmm” with your lips as relaxed as possible. Halfway (or so) through the out-breath, open your lips and change the ”mmm” smoothly to an “aah” sound – so it sounds like you saying “Ma” (only much longer). Repeat this for all the vowels*: May, then Me, then My, Moo.
3 Say “Hello”, then “Hellolololololololo”, with “los” repeated as quickly as you can.
4 Try some of the tongue-twisters on page 28.

* Vowels are the letters A, E, I, O, and U. At least one of these letters appears in every word, and they are the open sounds that link together the other letters, called consonants. To say consonants you have to use your tongue. Vowels mean just changing the shape of your mouth, and you should try to get them as open sounding as possible – so that your breath is coming straight up your throat and out in as controlled a way as possible.

Tongue twisters

People have always enjoyed tongue twisters. Some are as old as English, but new ones are being made up all the time. You can find loads on the Internet or make up your own. Here are some to get you going. Repeat them as quickly and perfectly as you can.

- Charlie's chic chip shop sells chilly cheap chips. (Careful not to say "ships" instead of chips.)
- Red lorry, yellow lorry, red lorry, yellow lorry.
- Six slippery snails, slid slowly seaward.
- A bloke's back bike brake block broke.
- Can papa pop a proper cup of coffee in a proper copper coffee pot?

Some tongue-twisters have been made into little poems:

She sells sea shells on the sea shore.
The shells that she sells are sea shells I'm sure.

A flea and a fly flew up in a flue.
Said the flea, "Let us fly!"
Said the fly, "Let us flee!"
So they flew through a flaw
in the flue.

A skunk sat on a stump.
The skunk thunk the stump stunk,
And the stump thunk the skunk stunk.

Here's a really tricky one:

She is a thistle sifter
and she has a sieve of sifted thistles,
and a sieve of unsifted thistles,
and the sieve of unsifted thistles
she sieves into the sieve of sifted thistles,
because she is a thistle sifter.

3 Working together

All the exercises in the last chapter you can do entirely by yourself, if you want. But it's much better to get together with other actors if you can, and the activities in this chapter you can only do in a group. Either join a proper class or acting group (*see 'Want to know more?'*) – or get together with a few friends. You don't have to have a theatre, or even a proper rehearsal space. All you need is a reasonably big bedroom or living room – or even a garage – where you can make a bit of noise and clear the furniture out of the way. Designate someone as group leader for each session. And keep sessions brief at first – no longer than 45 minutes, then build up to longer times when you're into the swing of it.

Ready to rehearse

Playing games

When you start to act, or get together with other actors for the first time, you're all bound to feel a little inhibited. There is no better way of getting over this initial barrier than to play games.

The right games not only help actors relax; they also help build up the trust between them that is essential for good teamwork. They can even help the actor develop particular skills. Some theatre directors believe games are such a good way for actors to work together that they base many of their rehearsals around games.

- **Breaking the ice** Games of Tag are a great way to get rid of excess energy and get everyone used to physical contact. Everyone knows their own game of Tag. But you could try Statues. In this, one person is 'It'. Whenever anyone else is touched by 'It', they have to stand still as a statue with their legs apart – until someone releases them by diving between their legs. 'It' has to turn everyone into statues. Another game is Chicken Run. One person starts as 'It' in the middle of the room. The others line up against one wall. When 'It' shouts, "Chicken!" they must all start to run to the other wall before 'It' counts slowly to ten. They are safe once they touch the far wall, but if 'It' touches anyone on both legs, they join 'It' in the middle. The game goes on until only one is left to run from wall to wall. The last person left becomes the new 'It' to continue.

Working together

- **Getting together** After the energy of Tag, a game of quiet concentration like Hand Telegrams is a good idea. Everyone sits down in a circle, joins hands and shuts their eyes (the game won't work if anyone peeps).
One person starts by gently squeezing the hand of his neighbour on the left. The neighbour instantly squeezes the hand of his neighbour on the left, and so on round the circle. The idea is to pass on the squeeze as quickly and quietly as possible. Soon it feels like a pulse drawing the group together. Once you get good, you can try a double pulse, or a pulse going round the other way – or one pulse going one way and another the other way at the same time.

- **Being aware** Hand Telegrams helps you develop the awareness you need to work well together in a group. You can take this a stage further with a game that sounds simple, but is not at all. The idea is to count to 20. With the group in a circle, one person says "One". Anyone else can say "Two"; you don't go round the circle in order. A third says "Three". And so on. If two people say a number at once, you must go back and start again quickly. Try getting someone to time the group doing this to see if your concentration is improving.

Developing trust

As an actor you sometimes have to make yourself very vulnerable physically or emotionally – so you have to be able to trust the other actors you're working with. There are many games to help develop at least physical trust. One of the simplest is with a blindfold. The group splits into pairs – the pairs preferably shouldn't be friends already. One of you puts on a simple blindfold. The other silently guides you round the room with just a light touch on the shoulder – tapping your right shoulder to go right, your left to go left and both to stop. If someone puts a few obstacles such as chairs and cushions on the floor to steer round, it makes it more of a challenge. It can be quite scary at first walking blind, but you soon learn to rely on your guide.

The Mirror Game

The Mirror Game is a game that almost every actor has played once or twice – and many have played it dozens of times – often without ever knowing why. The idea is that two people stand facing each other, quite close together looking into each other's eyes. One of them starts to make slow movements and the other person mirrors the movement exactly. The leader keeps his movements simple and smooth so that his partner can be a perfect reflection. What this does is take away some of the self-consciousness about moving your body by allowing you to concentrate on someone else's – but still keeping you in complete control. If you do feel self-conscious about moving around in a slow, controlled way in acting classes, try this game. If you ever feel really awkward about a move you have to do on stage, try asking someone else to lead you through it while you mirror.

Making it up

Sometimes actors do scenes and plays from scripts. Sometimes they are simply given a starting point and asked to make it all up as they go along. This is called improvisation or, as luvvies like to say, 'impro' or 'ad libbing'. This can be a frightening thing to do, and many actors, including some of the best, have found themselves frozen with fear and their minds going a complete blank. The box over the page gives an idea of the kind of things you might be asked to do.

Some actors swear by improvisation and say this way of working allows the actor to be genuinely creative and 'truthful' in their acting. Whole shows, called 'devised' shows, are often created by actors who have made it all up in rehearsals. Yet some actors hate improvisation and believe that it is a complete waste of time. They argue that it is the actor's task simply to make a script come alive.

But even actors who don't believe in making up whole scenes generally agree that even when using a script you need to work on the role without the script for some time to help make the role come fully alive. We'll come to this in the next chapter.

High and Low

Improvisation games can be a good way of exploring how people react together. One popular kind is 'status' games. These play on the idea that some people are leaders and some are followers. Actors are assigned different status numbers from one to ten, and asked to act a simple scene together using their status numbers.

Improvisation exercises

- *A classic impro exercise is building a human machine. One actor starts pretending to be a simple machine, such as a pump, making suitable noises. Then the others join in one by one, adding a new action and noise. The idea is to build a complete, whirring, hammering, squeaking machine.*
- *Another starts with the actors sitting in a ring. One stands in the middle and starts to mime a simple action, such as making a cup of tea, or opening a door. The others try to guess what he is doing. Once they guess, the group leader says "Freeze!" and the actor freezes. Another actor gets up and appears to join in the mime but actually creates an entirely new mime. He might take the imaginary cup, for instance, and turn it into an imaginary paintbrush. The first actor sits down. Once the others guess the new mime, the leader says "Freeze!" and a third actor takes over. The game goes on until everyone has created a mime.*
- *A more challenging impro is when the actors are each given a particular role or task, unknown to the others, and put in a particular situation – and have to make up the scene as they go along. One actor might be secretly told to be a strict headteacher. Another is told to go and see the headteacher as a pupil caught eating in class, then notices the head's face is covered in chocolate.*

4 Coming to your senses

When you stand up in front of people to speak or get on stage to act, it is only too easy to get shut off inside your own world. You start thinking so much about what you're saying and doing that someone could pour a bucket of water over you and you'd hardly notice. Actors often talk about being focused, but being focused does not mean shutting down your senses. This is the easiest mistake of all to make when you're acting, and it's surprisingly hard to beat – yet it's incredibly easy for an audience to spot. You may be so wrapped up in your part that you don't notice that you're drinking from the inkwell, but you can be sure everyone else will!

What you should aim for is to be thoroughly in control of what you're doing – yet totally responsive and alert to what is going on around you. An actor has to be more, not less, sensitive than other people to things happening and the activities in this chapter are designed to help you develop this sensitivity and responsiveness.

Granny's Footsteps

A good game for developing your senses – and also your body control – is Granny's Footsteps. One person is Granny and stands at one end of the room, facing the wall. The others have to creep from the far end to touch Granny on the back. Every now and then, Granny turns round suddenly. If she sees anyone moving – even a slight wobble – they are sent back to start again. Granny soon learns to sense when people are moving, and the creepers learn that perfectly controlled movements work in the long run.

Pinpoint memory

It is crucial when you're acting that you're conscious of yourself – not self-conscious and awkward but subtly aware of just what your body is doing and the sensations it is feeling. In real life, this comes quite naturally most of the time. The problem is that when acting it all goes awry because you're so worked up about some things that you forget about these everyday things.

The following exercise seems dull and easy at first sight. But the more you do it, the harder you realize it is – and the more interesting it becomes. Over a week, think carefully about everything you do when you go into the kitchen and get a coke or a glass of milk. The idea is to memorize every detail so precisely that you can recreate it perfectly in front of your acting group – without any props to help you at all.

When you come to do it in front of the others, first try to recreate in your mind the kitchen and everything in it as accurately as possible – and imagine it all completely in the space in front of you. Then try to recreate every single little movement in getting the drink – bending down, opening the fridge, getting a glass and so on – as accurately as you can. Get the others to tell you whether what you're doing looks completely real – and if they can be sure where everything in the kitchen is. Beware of being lazy – pulling a glass from waist height when it is really on a high shelf, or pulling it straight down off the shelf when really you have to slide it out a little way first.

If you're working by yourself, get a parent or friend to tell you how you're doing – or film yourself on video if you can.

Making an entrance

Coming on to the stage is called 'making an entrance', and there are all kinds of ways of making an entrance. You can swing in on a trapeze. You can glide in on roller skates. But most of the time, your entrance has to look as natural as you walking into your own bedroom. The audience has to believe not that you're an actor dashing on to a stage, but a real person coming into the place in which the scene is set.

Just as with the drink exercise before, you have to create the scene in your mind completely before you enter – and then enter it just as you would if the room were real.

- First practise making an entry into a room that you have created in your imagination. Get someone to watch you and tell you how convinced they were the room was real. Make sure you came through the door properly.
- Now, lay out a few props such as chairs, tables, books and so on to suggest the room you imagined. Try making your entrance again. Was it as convincing as before?

The secret is to be low-key and relaxed. All too many actors are tempted to 'ham it up' (overdo it) and it looks very unreal.

Coming to your senses

Once you believe you have mastered this, it's time to create a short scene. Finish the scene by 'making an exit' (going out of the room). Try these ideas:

- Come into your bedroom after a hard day at school.
- Come into your lounge on the day of a crucial exam.
- Come into the kitchen and find a dead cat on the floor.

Beware of hamming up the last one. Try to imagine as accurately as possible how you would react to finding a dead cat. Don't ACT it – try to imagine it as if it were really happening and no-one was watching at all. Actors call this 'being in the moment'.

Having a purpose

There is another crucial aspect to making an entrance as well as being in the moment. This is 'having a purpose'. Normally, when you go into a room you have a reason for going in – and when you act you must know just why you (in the part you're playing) are going in. We'll look at this again later.

5 Starting a play

Starting work on a play can be really exciting. You may not have been cast as the star of the show but every role in the play can be rewarding if you spend time and effort making it really effective. And if you are the star, your work is just beginning...

Your first task is to read the script – not just once, but again and again until you know it really well. Try to make sure you understand what is going on in every scene – especially the ones that you are involved in! Then make a simple plan of the script, scene by scene, and see if you can summarize in a few words what is going on in each scene, and where you enter and exit.

Reading the script

Reading a script can be frightening. It's never as easy to read as a book and there are often bits where you haven't a clue what's going on. Occasionally, it can be so frustrating you just want to say, "What a stupid, boring play!" and give up. Don't. Even the best plays are hard to read – because, of course, they are not meant to be read. A play is meant to be performed – and when a good play is performed well, it suddenly comes to life so thrillingly that you can't imagine how you ever thought it was dull. It is up to you as an actor to create that bridge between the lifeless script and the living performance.

If you do find the script intimidating, don't worry. Just be patient and go through it bit by bit trying to imagine what might be happening on stage at each moment. If there are bits you don't understand, ask someone – your group leader if you have one. If there are bits you can't get your head round at all, don't despair. Quite often, scenes that seem impossible to understand on the page suddenly make sense when you see them in rehearsal.

What to look for

- **Understanding** When you go through the script, make sure you understand all the words. If there is a word you don't know, look in a dictionary. If there is a chunk you don't understand, discuss it with your group leader, or make a guess.
- **Old plays** If you're doing an old-fashioned play, remember that words may have changed their meaning or are no longer used. (*See 'What's in a name?'* over the page.) Also, old words may not be pronounced quite the way you think they are, so check in a dictionary or ask.
- **Verse** Some plays, like most of Shakespeare's, are written in verse, like poetry. This doesn't always mean they rhyme, but the words have a regular rhythm. You can tell if a play is in verse because speeches are split into separate lines of much the same length, all beginning with a capital letter. If it is in verse, say the words out loud and listen for the rhythm.

What's in a name?

In Shakespeare's play about the ill-fated young lovers Romeo and Juliet, Juliet cries from her balcony, "Oh Romeo, Romeo. Wherefore art thou Romeo?" You might know that 'thou' is an old word for 'you' – and even that 'art' means 'are', not a painting. But you might think that when Juliet asks 'wherefore?' she means 'where?' and she is shouting, "Where on earth have you got to, Romeo?" because he's missed their date. Actually, 'wherefore' is an old word for 'why'. So she is really asking, "Why are you called Romeo?" – not because she thinks it's a silly name, but because her family and his are in the midst of a deadly feud, and if only he was from a different family, their love would run smoothly.

- **Stress** Look for the key words in every sentence, the ones you need to stress – usually the ones that tell you something new. In '*Julie is praying for the lead role*', you would stress 'praying' if we already know she is after the lead role (what's news is that she is praying for it): *Julie is praying for the lead role.* But if the news is that it is 'the lead role' she is praying for, you stress 'the lead role': *Julie is praying for the lead role.*

- **Hidden meaning** Most modern plays are written in simple everyday language. But often this has hidden meanings. A character called Jane might say simply, "My house is quite big". But underneath, Jane is saying, "Won't you visit me, sometimes, instead of always going to Sally's?" To spot these hidden meanings, which people sometimes call 'subtext', think not just about what your character is saying in every line – but why they are saying it.
- **Images** Often plays use images to help create a fuller picture, and you should look for these.

Stressful Shakespeare

With old plays like Shakespeare's, sentences are often so dense it is hard to work out what it's all about. A good tip is to find the key word in each sentence – the word to stress – then say it out loud. Often the key word is the verb (the word which says what the person or thing is doing). In Shakespeare's famous play King Lear, old King Lear is out in a storm and says:

"You cataracts and hurricanoes, spout
Till you have drenched our steeples, drowned
the cocks!
...And thou all-shaking thunder,
Strike flat the thick rotundity o' the world!"

You may only have a vague idea what this means. So look for the verb in each of the two sentences (ending in an exclamation mark). In the first sentence the verb is 'spout'. So spout is the word to stress. In the second, it is 'strike'. Say the two sentences out loud, stressing spout and strike and it sounds a little clearer. If you now also stress the subject of each sentence – 'cataracts and hurricanoes' and 'thunder' – it all begins to make sense. By 'cocks' Lear means the weathercocks on church steeples. So Lear is daring the wind and rain to drown churches right to the top and daring the thunder to knock the world flat.

Learning lines

To work well in rehearsals, and move about and interact easily, all of the actors in a play need to know their lines perfectly. So it is vital to learn your lines early on. But don't try to learn them before you've done at least enough rehearsal to know the play and your character well. If you learn lines too early, you can sound as if they've been learned like a recipe book, complete with mistakes. What's more, lines are much easier to learn once you understand them well.

Some actors find that recording their lines and cues on a portable cassette recorder helps them learn, because they can go on learning even while walking, having a bath and so on. Others like a friend to help them.

(From Macbeth)*

Right on cue

When you learn a part, you need to learn not only your lines, but your cues and your entrances and exits too. Cues are the last words someone else says before you speak or do something. You also need to learn them together with your actions on stage, and your goals and triggers (*see Chapter 7*).

6 Creating a role

After you've read the script thoroughly, and you think you know what the play is about, the hard work really begins. This is where you begin to turn lines on the page into a living, breathing person on stage.

Start by having a close look at the part you are playing – we'll call it 'she', for simplicity – and ask these questions:

- What is she doing at each moment in the play, whether speaking or not?
- What do you know about her? How old is she? Is she rich or poor? Is she happy or sad? Is she kind or selfish?
- What does she look like?
- How do other people react to her?
- Why does she do what she does?
- What is special about her?

Once you have answered all these questions, you can begin to build your role into a fully-rounded, believable and interesting character. Some of this can be done in rehearsal with the others, but you will need to work by yourself as well between rehearsals.

Playing a part is not just about saying the lines as effectively as possible. You have to turn your character into a breathing, moving person – who is fully alive and recognizable at all times, whether they are speaking or not. All the time your character is on stage, you have to be that person. But how do you go about turning yourself into that person?

The answer is that you have to use your imagination. You have to imagine yourself as that person as fully and completely as you can. If that sounds hard, it's because it is. But in this chapter, there are a few tricks to help you. You don't have to use all, or even any, of them if you can find a better way, but they may help you if you're stuck.

Research time

Many actors believe that research is a crucial part of their work on a role. They spend days going round libraries, talking to people and visiting places to find out as much as possible. With some roles, research is essential. If you are playing a doctor examining a patient, it clearly helps to know what a stethoscope is and what it does. Or if you're playing someone with a broken leg, you need to know how they walk, and what it stops them doing. Even if the benefits aren't so obvious, it is worth doing as much research as you can. While you're researching, you're thinking about the role and developing it in your mind.

Get an exercise book to keep your research notes and bits and pieces that will help inspire you. Find pictures of people who look as you imagine the character does and stick them in your book. Cut stories that give you ideas from newspapers and magazines. Look for bits of cloth and other things that help give you a feel of the character.

Like an animal

One of the most useful tricks for helping create a character is to look at animals. Every person has their own way of moving and behaving, and one of the hardest things you have to do as an actor is change your way of moving and behaving to match the character's. Occasionally, this will be really obvious – if the character has a wooden leg, for instance, or a very dramatic twitch. But most of the time, the characteristics are a lot more subtle. And this is where animals come in.

Think about your character. What animal does she most remind you of? Is she slinky and powerful like a panther. Or is she timid and nervous as a mouse? Or docile and stolid like a cow? See if you can find an animal that matches her. If you can't think of one instantly, try flicking through a book for ideas. Talk to the director about your choice.

Creating a role

Once you have decided on your animal, study it closely – thinking about the way it moves, what it does in different moods, how it reacts to other animals and so on. If your animal is in the zoo, ask someone to take you to the zoo so you can see it for real.

After you've studied your animal, go home and pretend to be the animal (in the privacy of your room!) for a while, mimicking as closely as you can the way it moves and behaves. See if you can gradually transform it into your character. Get up slowly and move around the room as the character while still retaining the movements of the animal. Try saying some of your lines from the play while still moving like the animal.

Now make the movements as human as possible, while still retaining the flavour of the animal. Practise this again and again in your room so that when you come to the rehearsal you move and behave this way as the character without even thinking about it.

Look for a likeness

Another trick you can try is to look at people around you. See if you can find someone who matches your view of the character. If your character is nervous and shy, look for someone who seems nervous and shy in the same way. If your character is bossy, find someone who seems bossy. They don't have to be doing the same job as your character or even be the same age. All you need is someone who looks right. If you can, study your subject and try to note how they move and behave. Then, back in the privacy of your room, try to mimic it as exactly as you can. Just as with the animal trick, try to subtly change this into your character, and work on the character using this as a base.

Dressing up

Every person has their own way of dressing, and dressing up is a good way of helping your imagination into the character. You don't need a full costume; indeed, one item of clothing might be enough to trigger your imagination. Nor does the costume need to be one you wear on stage. The idea is simply to help you develop the character in rehearsal. Of course, if you can work with your real costume, so much the better.

With historical characters, it's easy to work out what to wear. As a Roman soldier, you might wear things that would give you the feel of Roman sandals and a helmet. As a romantic heroine from the 18th century, you might wear something like a long, flowing cloak. With an ordinary modern character like a teacher or a bank clerk, it seems harder. Don't worry too much about trying to find a whole costume, just look for a few key items. The character might be someone who wears a particular kind of hat or jumper. But the best item of all to look for is the right pair of shoes. Shoes have a huge effect on the way you walk, and the way you walk helps you really get into the feel of the character. Are they more likely to wear trainers or high-heels, Doc Martens or brogues?

Look for little personal props too – such as a favourite pen or an old notebook, or a particular kind of bag.

At home

Once you feel you know your character well, you can build on what you've learned from animals, likenesses and costumes by imagining the character in a very ordinary situation. Imagine your character fast asleep on an ordinary day, then waking up and going through all the normal things they do when they get up. What do they do when they get up? Do they jump up brightly? Do they get out of bed the wrong side? Do they dress smartly or untidily? What do they think about?

When you finally begin to rehearse, try and remember what you've learned about the character and how they move and behave in as much detail as possible.

Looking deeper

Many actors find it helps to get to know a character really well. So once you feel you have the way your character moves and behaves pinned down, go back and look through the script and try and find as much as you can about them.

Then use your imagination to dig deeper and create as full a picture of the character as you can. What might have happened to her immediately before the play, for instance? What kind of background might she have come from? Might this have affected the way she behaves in the play? If her little dog got run over when she was younger, for instance, it might affect the way she behaves when a dog is let off the lead in the play.

To help formulate your answers, it might help to ask these questions:

- *Who?*
  Who is she and who does she know in the play, for instance? (Character.)
- *Where?*
  Where does she come from and where does she go? (Place.)
- *What?*
  What is she doing and what does she want to do? (Intention.)
- *When?*
  When is the play set and what has happened before she appears? (Circumstances.)
- *Why?*
  Why does she do what she does? (Motives.)

On the spot

Once you have got as far as you can by yourself, you could try putting yourself in the 'hot-seat'. The idea is that you sit yourself in the 'hot-seat' in the middle of your group. Then one at a time, the others ask you questions as the character – and you answer as the character, using the word 'I'. They start with simple questions such as "What is your name?" and "How old are you?" but they gradually probe deeper, asking questions, such as "Why did you betray your best friend?" (or something appropriate). But the questions should never get hostile. The idea is for the group to help you develop the character, not trip you up like a criminal in the witness stand.

Some actors find 'hot-seating' really exciting, because they get a buzz from coming up with answers quickly. Others find it confusing. You should use it only if you find it genuinely helps you develop the character. If you find the questioning is taking you down the wrong track, gently call a halt to the questions.

Stanislavski and his System

Many people have thought long and hard about acting, but only one has come up with a really detailed theory about how to do it – a Russian actor and director called Konstantin Stanislavski, who worked in Moscow at the turn of the 20th century. Today nearly every actor's training is influenced by the acting system he developed, and even those who disagreed with his ideas, like Bertolt Brecht, were often provoked by them. Many of the suggestions in this book are based on Stanislavski's ideas.

At the time Stanislavski was working, theatres used to churn out plays with stock sets, costumes and characters. Actors simply learned lines and played the same types in every play striving for effect with loud voices and big gestures rather than anything more natural or individual.

Stanislavski could see that there were a few great actors, but why did most actors fail most of the time? The reason, he believed, was that the actor is in such an unnatural situation on stage that he resorts to well-tried gestures and tricks. For Stanislavski, the answer was for actors to immerse themselves so fully in their characters that they forgot how weird it was to be on stage, stared at by loads of people.

First of all, he argued, an actor has to think deeply about their character and find out as much about them as possible from the play. He also has to research how a character like his might live and act. This is called 'given circumstances'.

Secondly, he has to try and find the inner feelings and motives of the character, because this is what really drives them. Of course, actors will not always have lived through the same things as the character, but they may be able to remember similar emotions and experiences. An actor should ask, 'If I was in this situation, how would I feel?' This, Stanislavski called the 'magic if'.

Thirdly, Stanislavski tried to develop a way of putting this into effect in the play:

- The first thing is to break the play down into short units, often a few lines, and analyze in detail why the character says what he says and just what he is trying to achieve. This is called his 'intention'.
- The second thing is to work out what the character's overall aim is in a particular scene. Every single line and gesture must fit this overall 'objective'.
- The third thing is for the character to develop a 'through-line' – a simple idea of the way the character's objectives develop through the whole play.
- Finally all the actors come together to work out their 'superobjective' – what they are trying to do with the play as a whole.

Stanislavski put his ideas into practice at the Moscow Arts Theatre which he co-founded, and which put on the first great performances of Chekhov's plays. Many actors who studied under him in Moscow spread his ideas abroad.

7 Getting into action

Now you've got the groundwork done on your character and you feel you know who he or she is, you can begin to put this into action in rehearsals.

'Action' is a key word because, more than anything, actors are meant to 'act' – that is, they do things. When the people in an audience see an actor on stage, they have no idea what he is thinking, they have no idea how he feels. All they can see is the actor doing something on stage. So as an actor you have to make everything you do on stage crystal clear, so that the audience can see exactly what's going on. Before you start to rehearse a scene, go through the script and make sure you know what you should be doing at every point – and do it as clearly as you can.

What do you want?

For actors, 'action' has come to have a second and more particular meaning. When actors talk about an action, they're not only talking about what they are doing in an obvious sense – like 'walking across the room' or 'picking up a glass'. They're talking about what the character is really trying to do. When the character is walking across the room, it may be that what he is really trying to do is get out of the room as quickly as possible. If the actor has this in mind, he will walk in a certain way – and react to the characters around him in a certain way. And if, when the character is picking up the glass, what the actor is really trying to do is hide her sadness, she will pick up the glass in a certain way, and again, react in a certain way.

Joining Up

A fun game to play with actions is Joining Up. You can play this in an ordinary room, or on a set you put together in the rehearsal room. One of the group decides on three simple actions to do in the room. You have to join them together into a sensible or interesting or funny story using only those actions – and those watching have to guess what the story is. Don't worry about using words. The story starts when you enter the room.

Your three actions might be 1) to open a drawer 2) drop a book 3) then dive behind the sofa. You could link this into a story by being a burglar trying to rob the place. You tiptoe into the room and open the drawer gingerly, then pick up a book and in your nervousness drop it.

Dropping the book makes so much noise you hear someone coming to investigate, so you dive behind the sofa.

If no-one guessed the story, try again, perhaps changing the story, until they do. What is good about this game is that it helps you be clear and simple in your actions. It also helps show you how simple physical actions can be linked by a particular goal.

Playing for goal

Sometimes, your character will be trying to do the same thing throughout the scene. More often, though, what they are trying to do will change from moment to moment.

- Look at each scene carefully and see if you can work out what your character is trying to do at every moment.
- Look for the trigger, too, which changes what they are trying to do. It may be that at the beginning of the scene, they are trying to get out of the room quickly – but then a gorgeous girl comes in and they are suddenly trying to get her attention. So the trigger for the new goal is the girl coming in.

- Learn by heart what these goals and triggers are and put them into action as you play the scene.

Once you have found all these short-term goals and triggers, see if you can find an overall goal for the scene, and for each major section of the play. If all this seems horribly complicated and hard work, it's worth making the effort. Once you've laid these foundations rehearsals will actually begin to seem quite easy and fun.

To see how this works, break down a short scene into goals and triggers and then try rehearsing it.

As if...

Playing for goals certainly helps steer your path through each scene. But just what does each goal mean to *you*? The goal in the play might be telling the king he's wrong. But if you have never told a king he's wrong, how do you know how to go after this goal? The answer is you try to find something you do know about that is likely to feel pretty much the same. In this case, you might think it's the same as charging into the headteacher's office and telling him or her all the things that are really bad about the school.

Look at each goal you feel you don't know much about and say to yourself: "It's as if..." and find your equivalent.

If your goal was, say, 'to clear your name', you might say to yourself "It's as if mum came in and found me holding the broken pieces of her best vase – when actually it was the neighbour's cat (now nowhere to be seen) that knocked it over".

Do you remember?

Back in the 19th century, a psychologist called Ribot suggested that our brains record every experience that has ever happened to us. And the right trigger – a touch, a sound and especially a smell – can bring an emotion flooding back. Ribot thought that similar moods merge together in our memories, so every time we have been in love, or angry, or afraid, all these emotions gradually blur into one in our memories.

When he was devising his System of Acting, the great Russian actor Stanislavski realized that this memory of emotions, which he called Emotion Memory, could be really useful to actors (*see p. 60*). All the actor has to do is work out what emotion is needed at a particular point in the play. He then searches his memory for a time in his life when he experienced a similar emotion. As he plays the scene, he remembers that time, and he goes through the emotion again.

Some actors find this technique very useful, and use it all the time. Others find it too vague and uncontrollable. But all actors draw on their own experiences when creating a part.

Old memory

Actors have been drawing on their own life experiences to create emotions on stage for thousands of years. Way back in the 4th century BC in Ancient Greece, an actor, Polus, was in the play Electra by Sophocles. At that time, the women were played by male actors, and Polus was playing Electra. At one point in the play, Electra is supposed to cry bitterly over an urn holding the ashes of her father, Orestes. So Polus took from the tomb the urn holding the ashes of his own son who had died recently, and used that on stage instead of the stage prop. So when it came to crying as Electra, he was crying in genuine grief for his son.

Getting to know you

Most of the ideas so far, you can do by yourself. But most plays involve more than one person and the way people relate to each other is an important part of the play. So the next step is to develop the relationships with the characters you are on stage with.

First of all, look at every single character you are on stage with and work out who they are and what you feel about them. Ask yourself what you want from each of them. Do you want one of them to like you? Do you want one of them to go away? Do you want to make one of them feel small?

Once you know what you want from each character, memorize it and bring it into play every time you do the scene. But the crucial thing in relating to the other characters on stage is not to be stuck in your own world but to listen. Be alert to what each of them is doing and respond to it. This way you all work together to create the scene. However well you are carrying out your own tasks, the scene simply won't work unless you interact fully.

As rehearsals progress, listen to and watch what the other characters are doing and develop your response. If you respond to another actor you give that actor more to work with – and so she, in turn, gives you more back.

8 Acting space

Theatres come in all kinds of shapes and sizes, from tiny, shabby spaces with room for no more than 20 people and a stage the size of your bathroom to grand theatres holding thousands.

In older style theatres, the stage is typically at the front, set behind a large frame called the proscenium arch, with curtains that open to reveal it at the start of the play. In many modern theatres, the stage is surrounded by the audience either on three of its sides (a thrust stage) or all four (in-the-round). There is no curtain, so the start of the play is signalled by the actors entering and the lights coming up.

In the days of Ancient Greece and Rome, 2000–2500 years ago, thousands of people went to see dramas in huge, open-air theatres. You can still see the ruins of some of these theatres today, and they look more like football stadiums with terraces than theatres. But they had a round stage in the middle and a high back wall through which the actors entered. The actors wore huge masks and often spoke at the top of their voices; there was often a large 'chorus' to comment on the action and drive it along.

PROSCENIUM ARCH THEATRE
Oh yes I did!
STAGE
Oh no you didn't!
SEATING

THRUST STAGE
Ah me!
SEATING
STAGE

THEATRE-IN-THE-ROUND
A horse, a horse! My Kingdom for a horse!
STAGE
SEATING

The actor's right (or is he?)

Like all places, theatres have their own jargon, and it's worth knowing at least the basics, whether you're acting in a proper theatre or your own improvised space.

The most important terms to know are all the positions on stage. First of all there is Upstage and Downstage. Downstage is the front of the stage. Upstage is the back. When you're further away from the audience than another actor, you're upstage of him. If you do mad rabbit impersonations behind him while he's doing his big tragic speech, you're said to be 'upstaging' him (and asking for trouble!).

Then there is Stage Right and Stage Left. These are just like left and right in real life. The problem is remembering just whose left and whose right. Stage Right is your right when you're facing the audience. Stage Left is your left when you're facing the audience. If you turn round and face the back of the stage, of course, Stage Right is your left and vice versa… The diagram should make it all a little clearer.

Fortunately, Centre Stage is just where you'd expect it to be.

Here are some other useful terms:

- *Wings*. These are the areas at each side of the stage, masked by curtains or flats, from which you make your entrance.
- *Rake*. This is when the stage slopes down towards the audience to help them see the actors better.
- *Fly gallery*. The grid, above the stage, from which things can be suspended over the stage or lowered on to it.
- *Pross Arch*. Short for proscenium arch.
- *Auditorium*. Where the audience sits.

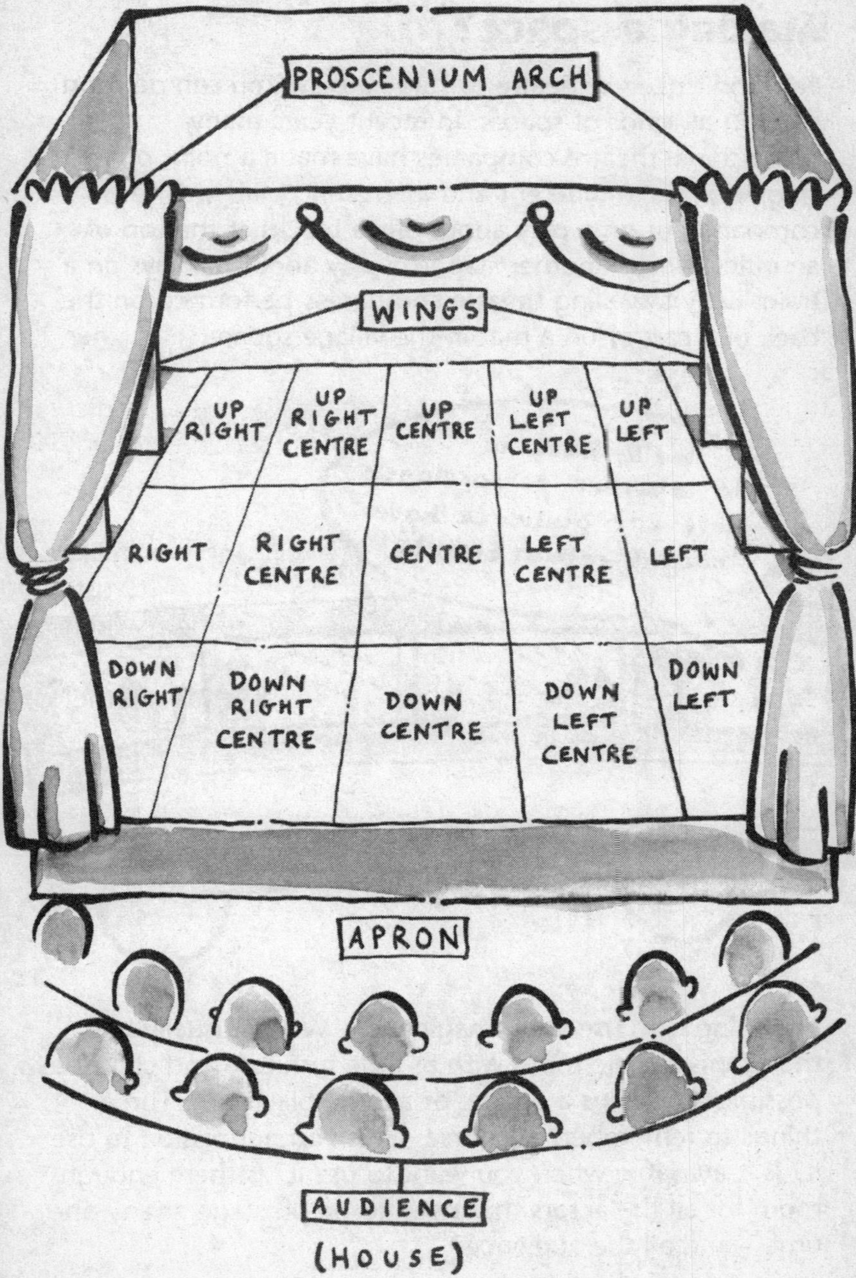
PROSCENIUM ARCH
WINGS
UP RIGHT
UP RIGHT CENTRE
UP CENTRE
UP LEFT CENTRE
UP LEFT
RIGHT
RIGHT CENTRE
CENTRE
LEFT CENTRE
LEFT
DOWN RIGHT
DOWN RIGHT CENTRE
DOWN CENTRE
DOWN LEFT CENTRE
DOWN LEFT
APRON
AUDIENCE
(HOUSE)

Making a space?

You don't need a theatre to stage a play. You can perform plays in all kinds of spaces. In recent years many professional theatre companies have made a point of staging plays in different and interesting places. One company put on a play about office blocks at the top of an office block. Another staged a play about railways on a train. Early travelling theatre companies performed on the back of a cart or on a mat in the village square.

The thing is to use your imagination. What's usually best, though, is a large room with as little furniture and clutter as possible – perhaps a garage or a large playroom. Three things to remember, of course: have you permission to use it? Is it available when you want to use it? Is there enough room for all the actors that need to be on stage at any one time – and all the audience?

If you are using a makeshift space, take the time to prepare it as carefully as possible. Set up chairs for the audience and move furniture and ornaments to give yourself a clear acting space. Arrange the room lighting to light the acting space and not the audience. If you can, arrange some curtains as wings from which the actors can enter. If this is impractical, arrange chairs around the side of the acting area. Actors can simply stand up when they have to make an entrance. This is much better and cleaner than trying to use a real door as an entrance.

Creating a set

The set is the scenery, furniture and other bits and pieces you put on stage to create the right environment for your play, whether it is set in a kitchen or on a planet in outer space.

You might think you need elaborate scenery to stage a play properly. But the idea of painted scenery came in only in the late 18th century, when skilled painters began painting wooden cut-out trees on the wings, and the wings got bigger and bigger until they took over the whole stage. In the days of Shakespeare, plays were performed on a bare stage with no scenery at all, and many plays today are performed on empty stages with very little scenery.

The runaway train

In the early 19th century, theatre scenery got more and more over the top. People didn't have cinema in those days, of course, so they went to the theatre to see all kinds of exciting special effects. Each play had to have its spectacle, whether it was a fantastically wet raging flood or a terrifyingly convincing runaway train. It was quite normal to have a few horses on stage or an elephant or two. Some theatres were able to stage full-scale naval battles – with real water, or switch from an erupting volcano to a quiet cottage interior in seconds as huge teams of stage hands hauled on masses of ropes and pulleys. When the composer Wagner staged the first performance of his vast opera The Ring of the Nibelungs in 1876, he had the great river Rhine overflowing its banks on stage, and the Palace of Valhalla come crashing to the ground.

It is often better to leave things to the audience's imagination. If your play is set in a palace, there is no way you can recreate this realistically, so don't even try. All you need are a few things to touch off the imagination – a big upright chair draped with a piece of velvet, for instance. Even the hints don't have to be realistic – as long as you make it clear that they are symbolic. You might suggest a vast forest, for example, with something as simple as a few broom handles mounted upright. Unless you have a good reason for being elaborate, keep things simple and unfussy, starting with the bare minimum and only adding things when you feel they are genuinely needed.

Acting space

Go through the play bit by bit, making a list of what you need at every point in the play. Then use your ingenuity to cut out as much as possible. Think of ways in which the same pieces of your set can be made to work as different things in different scenes. A handful of boxes might be chairs in one scene and a wall in another. One thing to pay particular attention to is scene changing. Audiences will get bored if you take even a few minutes to change scenes. Keep scene changes to a minimum, and make them as swift and easy as possible; or where appropriate, make them part of the action.

A backdrop of some kind helps, though, if you are playing 'end-on' – that is, with the audience facing you from one end of the room. If you are playing end-on, try to rig up a piece of suitable material to mask the back wall.

Man of vision

One of the most famous of all theatre designers was Edward Gordon Craig (1872–1966). He trained under the famous actor Henry Irving before turning to design. This may be why some actors said he was an actor manqué – which is ACTOR-speak for a failed actor – when he suggested the actors should do as little as possible on stage to avoid distracting from the set. In the 19th century, stage sets had all been terribly realistic, and many directors had competed with each other in getting their set absolutely authentic, right down to shipping in the right insects from thousands of miles away. Gordon Craig wrote a series of magazine articles in which he said you should get rid of this pedantic realism and replace it with arrangements of shapes and colours that created the mood and character of the place. Gordon Craig's ideas were hugely influential, but he only got the chance to put his ideas into practice once – for a production of Shakespeare's Macbeth in New York in 1928.

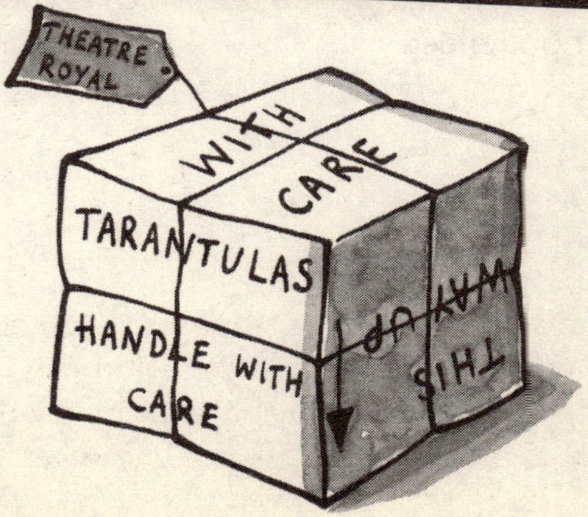

Designing a set

If you can, it is worth really thinking about the overall look or 'design' of your set. The set is often the first thing people see at the start of a play, and it sets the tone for the whole performance. Professional theatres employ designers to create an imaginative set that will have the right impact. But the set also has to be practical for the actors to work on, and stay within budget.

Most plays give a strong hint as to what the set should be like. A play might be set in 'a dilapidated room', for instance. The designer has to take notice of the hints and the demands of the story and discuss with the director what kind of set would achieve the kind of effect they want. Some sets are symbolic, using shapes, textures and colours that make the most of the play. Others are 'naturalistic' – that is, as life-like as possible. Some are simply acting spaces. Of course, the set has to work in the space the play is being staged in, and must allow the audience to see the play properly.

Designing a set takes a lot of thought, and a good designer will often research ideas, then try out sketches, different materials and colour samples to see which combinations achieve the right effect.

Model box

Once they have decided on a design, most designers build a 'model box' – a scale model of the set to show exactly what it will look like. This not only helps the designer and director decide whether it is right and what changes to make. It also helps highlight any problems with building the set, and just how easy it will be for actors to work on.

To make a model box, you need to measure out the dimensions of the stage as accurately as possible, complete with all the entrances and exits, draw it to scale on paper, then use the scale drawing to make a model in card. Make cardboard cut-outs of each of the actors to the same scale to get an idea of how they will look on stage.

You will need:

- *A tape measure*
- *Thin and thick card*
- *A ruler, sharp pencil, rubber and pen*
- *A set square for drawing right angles*
- *A craft knife and cutting board*
- *Glue*

9 Putting on the style

PROPS, COSTUMES AND MAKE-UP

Props

Props is short for properties, and props are all the little things you need on stage to tell the story and decorate the sets. Some props are virtually essential. It would be difficult to do a play which ends with the hero drinking a cup of poison if you don't have a cup. So the first job for the person in charge of props is to go through the play carefully and make a note of all the props that will be needed, scene by scene.

Many props can be found, borrowed, or even made with a little ingenuity. A few you may have to buy or hire, but this is expensive, so it is worth estimating how much you will have to spend right from the start, then making a budget which you stick to. Professional props people become adept at searching through junk shops and raiding their friends' cupboards to find hard-to-come-by props at no cost. If you borrow anything, be sure it is looked after very carefully and returned after the show.

Once you have acquired all the props and are ready to do the show, you must 'dress the set'. Dressing the set means arranging all the right props on the set to make sure it is absolutely right in every detail. 'Personal props' are the props the actor wears or carries on stage with them. Sometimes, these might be things such as a pipe or walking stick that the actor uses to help develop the character. Sometimes, they might be a part of the story line – such as a vital letter which is handed to the heroine. Props like these should be laid out carefully on a 'props table' off-stage so the actor knows exactly where to find them.

Props for Cinderella

Costumes

You can manage without a set. You can even manage without props. But costumes are essential (unless you're doing a play about Adam and Eve, of course). Even if you don't wear costumes specific to the play, you need to choose what you wear carefully. Your own ordinary clothes give messages that may not be appropriate for the character. Also, you need a costume to help you step in your imagination from the everyday you to the role you are acting. So even if you decide not to bother with 'proper' costumes, at least make sure everyone in the cast wears some kind of stage uniform – perhaps black T-shirt and loose black trousers or skirt.

It is worth taking care over costumes. They not only affect the way actors move and feel, but their style helps identify characters and create the right atmosphere. Historical costumes set the piece strongly in its time. Set designers very often design the costumes as well, since they are so crucial to the overall look of the production.

When deciding on the designs do plenty of research, photocopying and drawing pictures from books and from the Internet – not only for ideas, but to make sure historical costumes are accurate.

Putting costumes together

In professional companies, once the costumes are decided, the 'wardrobe mistress' takes over and finds, makes or hires the costumes. Amateur companies generally hire more elaborate costumes – especially historical costumes – from costume hire stores. But professional companies typically make them afresh because it is very hard to find a complete set of hire costumes to match the designer's idea. But even the professionals usually have a limited budget, so wardrobe mistresses are adept at seeking out bargains and cheap alternatives at jumble sales and so on.

If you can neither hire nor find anyone to make new costumes for you, use your ingenuity to adapt existing old clothes, old bits of cloth or clothes picked up in a sale for next to nothing. You might be surprised just how effective such makeshift costumes can be with a little time and trouble. Here are some hints:

- To make period shoes, stick appropriate-looking scraps of material on a thin old pair of slippers, and add things like ribbons or buckles (made from foil-covered card).
- Old curtains and chair covers make good heavy materials for rich historical costumes.

Putting on the style

- Glueing cheap braid and adding ribbons is a cheap and effective way of making a costume, such as an old full skirt, look very fancy.
- Old velvet curtains make good capes – especially if you finish them off by glueing braid along the edges, and adding a strip of silk tape or ribbon to tie them.
- Large, old white cotton shirts can have the collars and buttons cut off (and sewn up) to make period blouses.
- Old raincoats can be cut short and adapted to make 18th century jackets (with the addition of cuffs made from cheap lace and big pockets made from the cut-off).
- Glue on decoration for a luxury look – or draw decorations in glue and paint the glue with gold or silver paint.

- Adapt old hats by sticking on ribbons and feathers.
- Dye things in a washing machine to the right colour.
- If a costume looks too smart and new for the character (if the costume is yours) you can 'break it down'. Attack it with a cheese grater at places where it is likely to wear, such as collar, cuffs and elbow, and make it dirtier by staining it with tea bags or mud.

Make-up

Actors used to work in such big theatres in such poor or unnatural lighting that they all wore incredibly heavy make-up – make-up so heavy that close-up it looked as if they'd fallen over in the mud. Nowadays, fortunately, theatre lighting is much better, and audiences sit closer, so actors wear lighter, more natural make-up if they wear make-up at all. Most film and TV productions have a make-up artist to make sure the actor looks good on screen, but many theatre actors do their own, and are very skilled at it.

Applying make-up well takes a great deal of practice, so unless you are good at it, it is best to get someone who is to do it for you. If you are acting in a small space, it is probably better to dispense with make-up altogether.

10 Jobs

You can put on a play with just a few actors, but most productions involve a whole team of people. There are all the people who design and build the set and those who find and make costumes and props. There are those who set up the theatre and arrange the lights and sound. There are those who publicise the show, sell tickets and look after the audience. And then there is the director…

The director

The director is the boss of the production. In the past, there was no such thing as a director. Theatre companies in the 18th and 19th centuries were usually run by the leading actor, who was called an actor-manager. Now actor-managers are very rare, and in most theatre companies it is the director who is in charge.

The director chooses the play, decides how to approach it and who will play all the roles (sometimes with the help of a casting director). The director tells the designer what kind of design is needed. And the director leads the actors through all the rehearsals, guiding them to achieve the effect he or she wants.

Different directors have different styles, and different ways of rehearsing. Some believe in letting the actors go their own way and simply helping them along. Others treat the actors like puppets, telling them exactly how to move and say things. But most come somewhere in between.

You can work as actors by yourself, but it really helps to have a director who can tell you what the play looks like and sounds like from outside, from the audience's point of view. It helps too to have a director to guide rehearsals and free you to concentrate on your role. If you do not have a director available, get one of the actors who has a very small role to lead you through the rehearsals, even if you all share in choosing the play and the approach.

The stage-manager

The stage-manager or SM does a lot more than manage the stage. In fact, managing the stage is just about the only thing the stage-manager doesn't do – that's left to the deputy stage-manager (DSM). The stage-manager's job is to do all the practical things needed to get the show up and running. The main task is to liaise with the designer and director before the performance and get the set built right. He also ensures the props person is properly briefed. He will also take charge of the final rehearsals in the theatre and make sure everything is in the right place – including the actors.

An assistant stage-manager (ASM) helps the stage-manager – typically getting the set and props in place.

The deputy stage-manager

The DSM's task is to 'run' the show. She works with the other production crew, she attends every rehearsal, and makes sure the actors know which rehearsals they need to attend. During rehearsal she notes down the planned movements of the actors on stage, all the props they will need and when, when scenery needs to be moved and so on, gradually building up all the material she needs to prepare 'the book' (*see p.92*). During performances, the DSM sits on the side of the stage or in the lighting box and uses the book to run the show. She has a small light so she can read the book, and a microphone linked to the lighting and sound people, backstage crew and the actor's dressing room. As the show progresses, she warns lighting and sound, backstage and actors that they have 'a cue' – that is, something to do – then tells them when to do it.

DSM
Lx Cue 49 to go!

Making a book

The book is the complete instructions for the show. It is mainly intended for the technicians, but often also includes details of where the actors should be on stage at a particular point in the play. To make a book, you need a copy of the play printed on one half of the page only and firmly bound. Go through and divide the blank side of each page with a line down the middle. One column is for backstage instructions and actors' moves*. The other is for LX cues. This is the most important one. LX is short for electrics, and is basically jargon for lighting and sound. If you hear a DSM during a show whispering in to her microphone, "LX cue 49 go!" she is telling the lighting (or sound) operator to put the 49th lighting change in the show into effect. During rehearsal, you write all the backstage instructions and the actors' moves* in the appropriate column on the blank page that is open opposite where they occur in the play. Draw a ruled line from the point where they occur in the play to each written instruction. Use pencil because there are bound to be changes during rehearsal. Towards the end of rehearsals, when the show is taking shape, do the same for all the LX cues, numbering them in order through the show. Remember, you need an LX cue for every single <u>change</u> during the show. That means you need a cue number for when a set of lights go off as well as when they go on. After the final technical rehearsal (*see p.110*), you can go over the pencil marks in ink.

*Use abbreviations for Upstage (U), Downstage (D), Left (L), Right (R) and Centre (C). You can abbreviate the names of characters, too. So if the actor playing Julie (J) is to move to the front of the stage in the middle, you would put, 'J to DC'. (Short for Downstage Centre.)

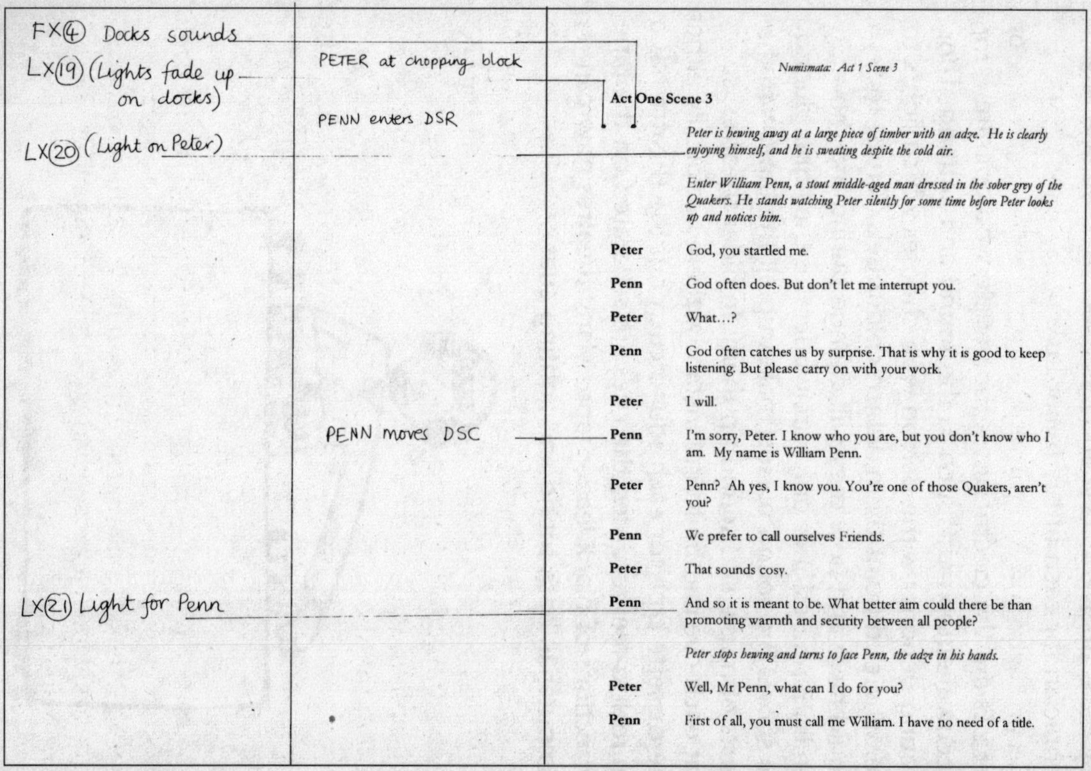

FX④ Docks sounds
LX⑲ (Lights fade up on docks)
LX⑳ (Light on Peter)
LX㉑ Light for Penn

PETER at chopping block
PENN enters DSR
PENN moves DSC

Numismata: Act 1 Scene 3

Act One Scene 3

Peter is hewing away at a large piece of timber with an adze. He is clearly enjoying himself, and he is sweating despite the cold air.

Enter William Penn, a stout middle-aged man dressed in the sober grey of the Quakers. He stands watching Peter silently for some time before Peter looks up and notices him.

Peter God, you startled me.

Penn God often does. But don't let me interrupt you.

Peter What…?

Penn God often catches us by surprise. That is why it is good to keep listening. But please carry on with your work.

Peter I will.

Penn I'm sorry, Peter. I know who you are, but you don't know who I am. My name is William Penn.

Peter Penn? Ah yes, I know you. You're one of those Quakers, aren't you?

Penn We prefer to call ourselves Friends.

Peter That sounds cosy.

Penn And so it is meant to be. What better aim could there be than promoting warmth and security between all people?

Peter stops hewing and turns to face Penn, the adze in his hands.

Peter Well, Mr Penn, what can I do for you?

Penn First of all, you must call me William. I have no need of a title.

Sample page from a 'book'

The backstage crew

The size of the backstage crew varies according to the size of the production. Often small companies have just one DSM who does just about everything. Larger companies not only have an SM, a DSM and lots of ASMs, they also have a technician for each of the major tasks.

The LXs are the electricians – the people who operate 'electrical equipment' such as the sound and lighting. The lighting designer is the person who chooses which lights to use, where to point them, which colour gels (filters) they should have and how they will change during the show. The lighting designer only rarely operates the lights during the show. The sound person makes up all the tapes with bursts of music and sound on them. In older theatres, so that each cue can be found instantly, there is typically either one cassette tape for each sound cue or, if the theatre has a big reel-to-reel recorder, the cues are separated on the tape by sections of blank leader tape. Many theatres now can computerize both sound and lighting cues.

Tekkies

Those who like to think they are in the know call the backstage crew 'tekkies', short for technicians. During a show, tekkies – if they exist – wear black and soft-soled shoes so that they make themselves as invisible and inaudible as possible to the audiences. At other times, according to legend, a typical tekkie wears loose T-shirt and faded blue jeans with a huge spanner in the pocket and an unfeasibly large bunch of keys dangling from the belt loop. Sometimes, the mythical tekkie can be seen emerging bleary-eyed after working in the theatre for 36 hours a day for five days solid, and shuffling off to the pub.

TV tasks

In television, jobs are very different from those in the theatre, and there are many more of them. Indeed the whole business of making TV drama is so much more complex than putting on a theatre play, that there is only room to give a quick rundown of the main jobs.

In TV, it is the producer who is usually the boss, not the director. Sometimes the producer is director as well, and even writes the script. It is the producer who gets the script, sets up the process of getting the programme made and hires all the staff, including the director. The director's task is to make sure everything goes to plan during the shooting and to make the script come alive.

Other team members include an art director who designs the settings, and craftspeople who build it; a costume designer; a props manager; plus a range of technical specialists who take charge of cameras, microphones, and lights. A production manager and a production coordinator make sure everything is in the right place at the right time.

Gaffers and others

Feature films have even more people working on them than TV dramas. As with TV it is the producer who is overall boss, and there is often more than one working on a film. But with films, the director plays a more pivotal role, because the shooting goes on for longer, and it is the director who controls how it is made. Indeed, many film directors, such as Stephen Spielberg, are as famous as the film stars who appear in their films.

Other crew members include the production manager who controls the money side and decides the shooting schedule. The director of photography achieves the look the director wants, supervising the camera and lighting crew. The art director co-ordinates the design of sets and costumes while the costume designer actually designs them.

Shoots begin early, and the technical crew typically arrives at six or seven in the morning to set up lights, cameras and sound. The director of photography gets electricians called gaffers to set up the lights. While this is all being readied, actors are putting on their costumes and having their make-up and hair done ready to start. They then have to hang around until everything is ready for shooting.

11 Putting on a play

If you belong to a drama group, the group leader will probably arrange each production, but if you don't – or even if you do – why not try putting on a play for yourself? Putting on a play is really exciting – and really, really stressful! Most people who put on plays find it a nightmare – then go on doing it again and again because it's all so thrilling. If you do put a play on yourself, the chances are there'll be times when you just want to run and hide and forget the whole thing. But when it's all over, you can't wait to do the next one.

There are three things to remember:

- Keep it as simple as possible.
- Get as much help as you can. Most people are only too willing to help out.
- Plan it all as carefully and in as much detail as you can, and give yourself ample time for preparation.

First, of course, you have to decide which play you're going to put on. Unfortunately libraries do not often have a very wide choice of plays, so you'll probably have to ask the librarian where you can get playscripts. Unless there is a particular

play you want to do, it's worth asking advice from a drama teacher. The important thing is not to be too ambitious. Choose a play that suits the talents and character of you and your company as closely as possible – and one that will be easy for you to stage. A play with lots of scene changes and special effects is probably a mistake, unless you have plenty of people to help.

When and where?

With your play chosen, you have to decide when to put on the play and where. We talked about the 'where' in Chapter 8. When it comes to the 'when', if you have a choice, give yourselves as much time as possible. It always takes longer to get a play ready for performance than you think it will. Professional companies typically have three to six weeks' full-time rehearsal time. But they usually know they are going to do the play and start preparing at least six months before. If you're doing a simple show at home, of course, you need much less preparation time.

To do a full-length play well, you probably need to do about 100 hours rehearsal. So work out how much time you can realistically devote to rehearsal each week, along with all the other things you have to do, including schoolwork and social time. Then divide this into 100 to find the number of weeks you need to rehearse for. Add twice the same amount of time again, allow a little more for unforeseen problems and you should have a rough idea of the time you need to get the play off the ground.

The check-list over the page gives an idea of the things you need to plan for.

Putting on a play

CHECK-LIST OF THINGS TO DO

GETTING STARTED

- Decide the play.
- Work out how long you need to get it ready.
- Decide the venue (where you're putting it on). Is the venue suitable for the play? Is it available on the dates you want? Are there any restrictions on your use of the space? Find out how much time you can have in the space for rehearsal and set-up.
- Work out how much money (if any) you have to spend. Prepare a budget.
- Decide who will take each of the key production roles. This will vary according to how many people are involved. If there are only a few of you, you may need to double up roles. But someone needs to take charge of each of these: set, costume, props, getting the show set up in the theatre, lighting and sound, safety checks, organizing rehearsals, preparing the book, controlling the budget, letting people know about the show (publicity), organizing tickets or guests, seeing the audience to their seats.

PLANNING THE PRODUCTION

- Read the script thoroughly and decide your approach.
- Decide how you want to stage it and what kind of set and costumes you need.
- Arrange a production meeting to plan all the tasks. Arrange to have regular production meetings every now and then.
- Agree on the design for set and costumes with the designer, the stage-manager and the costume maker/finder.
- Arrange a production meeting involving all the key people, including the stage-manager.
- Rehearsals: Find a suitable space to rehearse in and book it.
- Cast the show – that is, choose the actors for each role.

THE PRODUCTION PERIOD

- Arrange a schedule for preparing set, costume and props.
- Plan the lighting and sound.
- Work out a rehearsal schedule so that each scene in the play is fully rehearsed and send it out to all the cast and the stage manager.
- Get the publicity and guest lists under way.
- Get tickets made.
- Study the script and plan how each scene will work in as much detail as you can.

THE REHEARSAL PERIOD

- Introduce the cast and get them to read through the play out loud so everyone knows what's going on.
- Check at production meetings that set, costume, props and publicity are coming along – and all is within budget.
- Use the time between each rehearsal to plan the next in detail, learning from each as you go along.
- Make sure all actors know exactly where they should be at any time in the play.
- Make sure all the props they need will be found.
- Arrange time for actors to try on costumes.

THE FINAL COUNTDOWN

- Hold a production meeting to make sure that set, costumes, props will all be ready in time for the first rehearsal in the space.
- Check that the stage-manager has planned the 'get-in' – setting up everything in the theatre in detail.
- Do the get-in, put up the set, rig the lights and sound and make safety checks.
- Technical rehearsal for the technicians' benefit.
- Last-minute preparations.
- Dress rehearsals.
- First night.
- Sleep.

Rehearsals

Every director has his or her own way of rehearsing, but the more thoroughly you prepare the better. Study the script and make sure you understand what is going on in each scene and what makes each character tick. Then work out what you want to achieve with each scene in the play and try to imagine how you can do this.

Some directors plan everything the actors will do. Others simply provide a general framework and let the actors create scenes themselves, and most actors prefer this. Whichever approach you choose, it is worth visualizing scenes and working out how the actors might achieve the right effect so that you are ready with ideas to help them.

The first rehearsal is usually a read-through. This means the actors read the play out loud. Some actors are tempted to show off at the read-through, but this stops them (and everyone else) from listening properly to the rest of the play. It also encourages them to make hasty (wrong) decisions about how to say things. The read-through should not be a performance.

After the read-through, work with individual characters and scenes in detail. Concentrate on making the characters come alive and each scene tell a story effectively. Talk with the actors about their characters and agree with them about what they are doing in each scene. Aim for something simple and clear.

Get the actors to read through the scene you're working on first as a whole, then breaking it down into short sections. Make sure you understand every line: every line in a play has some purpose, so try to make sure that purpose is clear.

Work on each line until it sounds as if it is being said for real, for the first time ever.

Actors and directors are often tempted to do too much too soon, but you need patience. Let the actors explore their own feelings gradually, offer suggestions and hints. If they get stuck, try and find ways of helping them. A scene that an actor is finding hard to work on when sitting staring directly at another actor, for instance, may suddenly become easier if they sit facing the other way – until they are ready and comfortable enough to do the scene face to face.

Where to go

When the actors have begun to develop their characters fully, you can start staging the play. Measure out the stage and set as accurately as you can on the floor and mark it with masking tape. Then arrange the main bits of the set in place using handy substitutes – like an old kitchen chair for a throne, and so on. Mark the position of each bit of the set on the floor with tape. This way you can be sure it is in just the right place in every rehearsal.

Give the actors time to get to know the set, then gradually work through with them how they will move on stage. Some moves are written in the stage directions to the play, but the others must be worked out in rehearsals.

In the past, directors used to 'block' each scene in fine detail. Blocking means where and when characters will move on stage. The idea was that actors had to be told where to go so they created effective groupings on stage and never blocked the audience's view of another actor. Nowadays, a director typically gives the actors some general moves to get the scene going – then the actors and director develop more precise positions during rehearsals. The idea is to find what looks and feels right, but also what makes sense for the characters and achieves the right effect.

Putting on a play

The director needs to be full of ideas and suggestions for new and exciting movements and gestures that will help the actor achieve what he or she wants. A scene in which a character speaks his thoughts to the audience might seem silly and over the top when he stands talking directly to the audience. But if he is making a sandwich at the same time, it might seem easy and natural. You would probably be surprised at the extraordinary amount of thought that goes into every single moment of the play to make it work well. The important thing is to keep in mind just what the characters are trying to do and what effect you want from the scene.

Moving on

The first third of rehearsals is about discovering and developing the characters and scenes and establishing just what you are trying to do. After this, the actors need to learn their lines quickly and thoroughly – and then keep going over them until they know them so well they don't even have to think about what comes next. Only once they know their lines completely can they begin to concentrate properly on moving around on stage and making the character work.

Fastest play in the West

One technique many directors and actors use to make sure they know the lines perfectly without thinking is to do a 'speed run'. For this everyone sits around on ordinary chairs and speaks through the play as fast yet clearly as they possibly can. There should be no attempt to act. The idea is to get the lines said very fast and absolutely word perfect.

The second third of rehearsals is getting the play 'on its feet' – that is getting the actors moving about the stage, and learning all the 'stage business' – how to do everything from simple things like opening a letter to complex things like a fight. After each rehearsal, the actor needs to go over the moves and stage business in each scene again and again, so that like the lines, they can do them without thinking.

The final third of rehearsal is by far the hardest. This is the time when you actually have to make the scenes work. Now everyone should be able to run through the scenes like clockwork, with only the occasional mistake. But the scenes may be lacking life and excitement. What you must do is work on making every scene buzz.

This is the most frustrating time for both actors and directors. It can sometimes seem impossible to make scenes really work, and often everyone starts blaming everyone else. The director mutters about the poor actors he has to work with. The lead actor has a tantrum. The actors in smaller roles are convinced they could do it all much better. And everyone decides it's a rotten play by a rotten writer.

There is no easy way round this. If there were, it would all be rather dull. But it's crucial to remain calm and patient, and focus on trying to create that buzz in every scene.

Towards the end of rehearsals, you need to start making not just individual scenes work, but the play as a whole. Run the play through and discover whether the story is coming across clearly, whether the pace is interesting and varied and if the climaxes come when they should. It often helps to have someone watching who hasn't been involved in rehearsals.

But I'm the STAR!
But I'm the DIRECTOR!

Final countdown

At last, the time will come when you move into the space where the play is to be performed – unless you are lucky enough to be rehearsing there already.

The first stage is the get-in, when the technicians get the set erected on stage, the lighting person rigs the lights, and everything is put properly in place for the performance. This often takes at least a day, and often involves the technicians working late into the night.

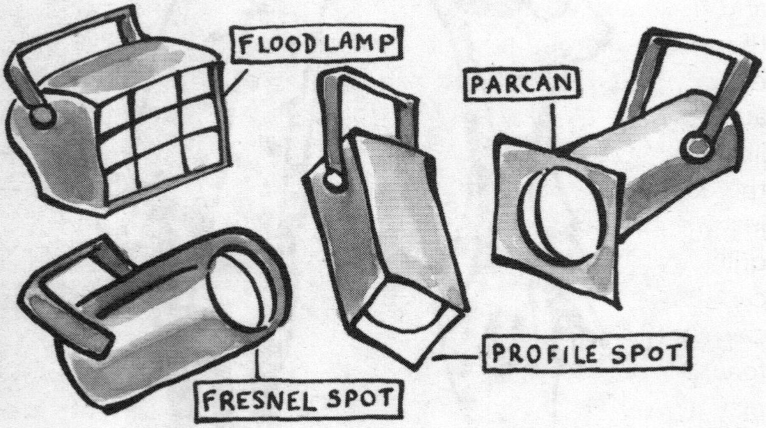

The second stage is the technical rehearsal. This is the first rehearsal on the set, but it is not for the actors; it is for the technicians. The idea is that the actors in full costume walk through the play so that the technicians can work out all their cues and make any adjustments needed. The technical rehearsal can often take many hours and can be incredibly boring for the actors, who often have to repeat the same action again and again while the director and technicians make sure the cue is exactly right. Sometimes, the technical rehearsal is 'cue-to-cue' which means the play is not run in full. Instead, it jumps from one technical cue to the next. Typically a full day is allowed for the technical rehearsal.

Once the technical rehearsal is done and the technical crew is happy that they can run the show smoothly, you move on to the 'dress rehearsals'. This is when the actors perform the play as if for real, with actors running through the play in full costume exactly as they would if an audience were there. The first dress rehearsal is typically on the third or fourth day after the start of the get-in. It is essential to have at least two dress rehearsals, preferably on separate days.

Finally, perhaps on day five or six, the first night arrives. First night is nerve-racking and exciting at the same time, and most actors prefer to spend the day relaxing rather than cramming in last-minute rehearsals. It is natural for everyone to be nervous when the show goes in front of an audience for the first time, and quite often actors forget lines they have been saying perfectly for weeks, or trip over the edge of a carpet. If this happens to you, don't panic – just forget it and go on with the play as smoothly and quickly as you can. Keep as calm and focused on the play as you can, even when you're off stage for long periods… and try to enjoy it.

12 On camera

To act on film and television, you need the same basic skills as you do to act in plays for the theatre. But because you are performing for a camera or several cameras, not a live audience, there are real differences.

One key difference is that your whole performance must be much more subtle and restrained than in a theatre. In a theatre, you need to fill the space so that everyone in the theatre sees and hears what you are doing. But with film and TV the camera brings you so close that even a twitch of the eyebrow becomes glaringly obvious.

A second major difference is that in the theatre, you rehearse for a long time then perform again and again, starting the story at the beginning then going right through to the end each time. In film and TV, you have much less rehearsal time – if any – and you may work on the closing scenes first, then scenes from the middle and then some scenes from the opening and some from the end. In fact, you do them in any order that makes production sense. You may also do just short sections of scenes, or even single lines, and the scene is completed only in the editing room.

Unlike plays, film and televison acting involves long days, usually starting early in the morning. The actor has to be around and ready to perform instantly throughout the day – yet may only be acting for a few minutes. The rest of the time is spent waiting for the crew to set up the shot.

One other major difference between film and theatre is the role of the director. In theatre, the director leads rehearsals, but then hands over to the actors entirely during the performances. In film, the director is in control all the time – not only while the actor is acting but afterwards too, choosing different camera angles, and splicing different scenes and shots together to build up the performance he wants. This way a good director can often make a terrible actor look brilliant – and a bad director can make a brilliant actor look terrible.

The Method

No approach to acting is more famous than the Method, followed by actors such as Marlon Brando in the 1950s, and later taken up by other American film actors like Robert de Niro and Al Pacino. Brando became so good at mean and moody characters from the low side of town who muttered and mumbled that even today many actors are convinced that this is what acting and the Method is all about. The Method was developed by Lee Strasburg, an actor who studied at the American Laboratory Theatre and was inspired by Stanislavski's system *(see p.60)**. The idea is essentially that the actor finds out so much about the character that he virtually lives the character's life during the rehearsal and performance period. This way, there is no need for the actor to 'act' in the role; they simply do what comes naturally. This Method works well in film and TV, where actors have to go into a scene at any point in the story at the drop of a hat, and where a low-key life-like performance is essential.*

Takes

Shooting a scene for film is usually called doing 'a take' and the actor is often thrown into a take without any preparation time. They may even have only got the script the night before. It costs money to pay actors to rehearse, and for most film makers it is simply not worth it.

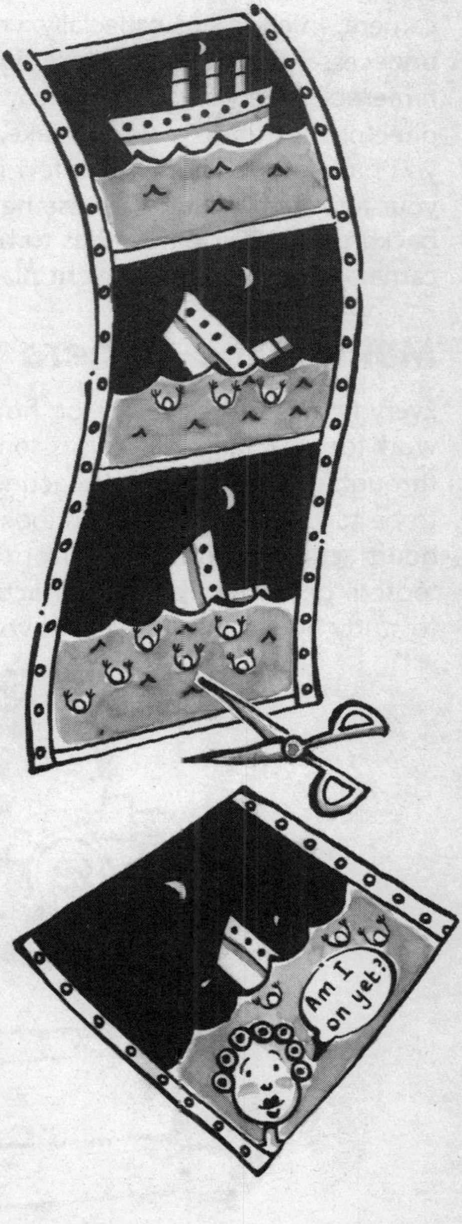

You have to be able to learn short sections of scripts very, very quickly. An actor who walks on to a film set with a script in his hand saying he hasn't had time to learn it is not likely to last long in the film business. You also have to be able to concentrate instantly the cameras start rolling. Film and film time is expensive, and no director wants to go through a scene again just because an actor wasn't quite ready.

Acting for film has to be precise in a way it never is for theatre. You have to direct your performance to a particular camera. In close-ups especially, you have to avoid every unnecessary movement. More significantly, you have to remember every single move you make precisely. When the director tries to do a second take, he does not want to find you have suddenly moved a few inches to the left so that your head is blocking the vase he wants to see in the background. Every move has to be inch-perfect so the camera keeps you in the right place in the frame.

Making the camera work for you

Every film actor has advice on how to make the camera work for you. But really this is something you can only learn through practice. In theatre acting it is probably a mistake to be too aware of what you look like. Actors who spend hours acting in front of a mirror tend to give unnatural 'posed' performances. But for acting on film, it really helps to study how every little move you make looks on camera.

A mirror gives the wrong idea – because it is almost impossible to see yourself as you are, but borrow a video camera and you can begin to study just what works and what doesn't. The idea of working with a video is to eliminate any obvious movements or poses and act as naturally as possible. The camera is so acute that it can see all too clearly when someone is posing for the camera.

You need to be aware of where the camera is all the time, but avoid staring straight at it unless this is specifically required. Let the camera see you, rather than you see the camera.

The future

What kind of plays and films and TV dramas people will see in the future depends on the actors, writers and directors growing up now – that is, you. It's up to you whether you follow the herd – or follow your own heart and head. Don't be in such a hurry to get on that you forget which one you've chosen. I know which I'd listen to.

Want to know more?

It is well worth joining a youth theatre group if you can. Here are a few useful contact names and addresses:

The National Association of Youth Theatres (NAYT)
Arts Centre, Vane Terrace, Darlington, DL3 7AX
The NAYT is an organization for youth theatre groups in England and Wales. As a young actor, you don't actually join the NAYT directly; the theatre group does. But it is a good way of finding out about just what is available.

Royal National Theatre Education Department
Royal National Theatre, Upper Ground, South Bank, London SE1 9PX
The UK's national theatre is a huge organization, and apart from staging plays in its theatres in London, it runs many schemes for young people, including the BT National Connections scheme (see p.120). Suzy Graham-Adriani is the Producer of Youth Theatre Projects there.

National Youth Theatre (NYT)
443-445 Holloway Road, London N7 6LW
Telephone for auditions: 0845 6039063
The National Youth Theatre is one of the country's leading youth theatre companies, founded in 1956. It is open to young people from 14-21 years old and each year 3000 audition for it in cities across the UK. Those who are successful then go for a summer course in London.

Scottish Youth Theatre (SYT)
6th Floor, Gordon Chambers, 90 Mitchell Street, Glasgow, G1 3NQ
Telephone 0141 221 5127   Fax 0141 221 9123
e-mail: admin@scottishyouththeatre.freeserve.co.uk
The Scottish Youth Theatre is Scotland's own theatre company for young people and performs and links in to schools all over Scotland.

National Youth Music Theatre (NYMT)
5th Floor, Palace Theatre, Shaftesbury Avenue, London W1V 8AY
Telephone 0207 734 7478
This is the theatre company for those who are interested in musical theatre. It stages many high quality productions and has shows written especially for it by top class writers.

National Youth Theatre of Wales (NYTW)
245 Western Avenue, Cardiff, CF5 2YX
Telephone 02920 265060
Wales's national youth theatre gives a number of young actors the chance to take part in professionally directed and produced drama in both Welsh and English language.

National Association for Youth Drama (NAYD)
34 Upper Gardiner Street, Dublin 1, Ireland
Telephone 01 878 1301
Organization for youth drama and youth theatre in Ireland. Members include over 60 youth theatre groups.

Shopfront Theatre for Young People
88 Carlton Parade, Carlton, Sydney, NSW 2218, Australia
Telephone 02 9588 3948
Offers a programme of drama workshops in which professional tutors are available to help young people produce a performance.

Web sites

There is a huge and growing number of links on the Internet for youth theatre groups.

London Bubble Theatre Company
http://www.londonbubble.org.uk
London's Bubble runs the BYTe-Sized theatre for young people aged 11-14, which includes a 12-week acting skills course on Tuesday evenings.

NAYT
http://www.nayt.org.uk

Want to know more?

The National Association of Youth Theatre's web site.
BT National Connections
http://www.nt-online.org/youth/
The British Telecom National Connections scheme is a project in which ten top playwrights each year write plays for young people to perform simultaneously across the country. The web site tells you how the scheme works and gives you a taster with samples from the scripts. If you participate, you can get all the scripts online.

National Youth Theatre of Wales
http://www.wjec.co.uk.nytw.html

School Show Page
http://members.aol.com/theatreuk/main.htm
The School Show page is a big site run by Peter Latham that has hundreds of different things, including texts of plays suitable for young people.

Polka Theatre Company
http://www.polkatheatre.com/index2.htm
Polka is a long-established and popular theatre company that stages shows for young people and runs workshops.

Stage schools

There are many stage schools, schools where you go instead of going to an ordinary school. This is just a few of them.

The Italia Conti Academy of Theatre Arts
Italia Conti House, 23 Goswell Road, London EC1
Telephone 0207 608 0047
Anna Scher Theatre
70-72 Barnsbury Road, London N1 0ES
Telephone 0207 278 2102
Sylvia Young Theatre School
6 Rossmore Road, London NW1 Telephone 0207 402 0673
Arts Educational School
Cone Ripman House, 14 Bath Road, Chiswick, London W4 1LY
Telephone 0208 994 9366

Brief history of theatre

Although we know that the Egyptians staged plays and the Ancient Sumerians probably did too, it was the Ancient Greeks who really started it all. Greek actors wore huge masks and often spoke at the top of their voices, and there was often a large chorus to comment on the action. The Greeks and Romans performed comedies and also tragedies with terrible deeds and strong emotions. The first great writer of tragedies was an Ancient Greek called Aeschylus (pronounced EESS-ker-luss). Aeschylus (525-456 BC) is famous for three plays about the hero Orestes. Equally powerful are the dramas of Sophocles (497-405 BC, pronounced Soff-o-klees) and Euripides (485-406 BC, pronounced U-rip-i-dees, as in "You rip o' dees costumes and you pay for 'em!"). Sophocles' *Oedipus Rex* is about a king who unwittingly kills his father and marries his mother.

Shakespeare and Co

In the Middle Ages, early dramas were often religious and staged in churches. Mystery plays, for instance, told Bible stories in a dramatic and colourful way. But in the late 16th century, people began to write and stage plays about real people – especially in England and Spain – and with these plays came the first real theatres.

In England, there were theatres called 'wooden-Os', like the Globe Theatre in London, which has recently been reconstructed. Wooden-Os were round wooden buildings with the stage and audience in a pit in the centre, open to the sky. Here, noisy crowds watched the first professional actors perform dramatic new plays by playwrights like Christopher Marlowe (1564-1593), Ben Jonson (1572-1637) and, of course, William Shakespeare, who wrote such famous plays as *Hamlet* and *Romeo and Juliet*. In Spain, people crammed into open courtyard theatres called 'corrales'. This time is called the 'Golden Age' of Spanish drama, for thousands of often wonderful plays were written and performed. The best writers were Caldéron de la Barca and Lope de Vega (1562-1635) who wrote such brilliant plays as *El Perro del Hortelano (Dog in the Manger) and El La Dama Boba (The Silly Girl or Mad for Love)*. While there were no actresses in England, and all the women's parts were played by young boys, in Spain, there were women in all the main theatre companies, and so roles were written to suit them.

Wigs and frocks

Many early plays were about heroes and kings and were set in exotic locations. In the late 1600s, people like the great French comedy writer, Moliere, and English writers like Dryden and Farquhar and later Sheridan and Goldsmith, began to write comedies poking fun at ordinary upper class people. In these plays, the actors wore clothes no different from the audience – except more flamboyant. Men in wigs and women in frocks strutted around the stage being very witty or very vain. The plays were often rude, and many actresses were regarded as little more than prostitutes. So theatres frequently ran into problems with the censors.

Getting real

In the early 19th century, towns and cities grew huge, in Britain especially, as the Industrial Revolution got under way – and all the factory workers and the new middle class flocked to giant new theatres. Theatre companies staged plays with adventure stories and all kinds of dramatic special effects to keep audiences entertained. Actors got more and more over the top and careless just to compete with the crashing volcanoes and collapsing buildings. Some playwrights like the French writer Eugene Scribe churned out literally hundreds of plays to the same formula to keep the theatres busy.

But towards the end of the 19th century, some writers began to get bored with this approach and felt that theatre could be far more realistic. Dramas could be about real people facing real situations, and characters in plays need not be like cardboard cutouts but fully rounded people with inner feelings and psychological depth.

Perhaps for the first time in the history of drama, European playwrights began to write not about heroes and villains, victims and vamps, but ordinary people living ordinary lives. In Norway, Henrik Ibsen (1828-1906) began to write about the relationships of the middle class in plays like The *Doll's House* and *Ghosts*. In

Sweden, August Strindberg made a powerful drama of child custody in *The Father*. In Russia, Anton Chekhov (1860-1904) wrote complex, involving plays about the dispiriting lives of Russian families, as in *The Seagull*. These plays were often staged in small, studio-style theatres where the audience were intimately involved and could see every little gesture. To go along with these new plays a new style of naturalistic acting developed.

Kitchen sink

Playwrights like Ibsen, Strindberg and Chekhov wrote about real people, but people who were upper or upper middle class. The working class – in other words, all but a few people – were never seen on stage except as servants, messengers or soldiers. But in the 1940s and 1950s, in America and Britain, playwrights finally began to write about situations so down-to-earth that they got the name 'kitchen sink' dramas, because it almost seemed as if they were set round the kitchen sink rather than in a posh drawing room or grand battle.

There were outsiders too, who were taking drama in an entirely new direction. Samuel Beckett, for instance, was able to write plays in which two people talked to each other from dustbins, or simply talked while waiting for something to happen (in *Waiting for Godot*).

Up to date

Today's more established playwrights, like Tom Stoppard, David Hare and Alan Ayckbourn, are often writers who made their names writing clever, witty plays like Stoppard's *Jumpers* or social comment like Hare's *Pravda*. Some younger playwrights, on the other hand, get their inspiration from film and TV or youth culture, writing plays full of fast-talking weirdos and screwed up babes.

Glossary

Apron The part of the stage that extends into the auditorium

Auditorium The area where the audience sits

Backstage The part of the theatre behind the stage. This includes dressing rooms and the area where the actors wait before going on stage

Border Curtain used to hide lights

Curtain call When the actors come on stage for applause at the end of the show

Front-of-house The theatre in front of the stage. Front-of-house staff are those who deal with the audience, selling tickets and ushering them to their seats

FX Short for sound effects

Green room The room backstage where actors sit around

Grid The steel framework above the stage from which lighting and stage equipment is hung

House lights The lights in the auditorium for the audience

Impro Short for improvisation. Creating a play or scene spontaneously without a script

LX Short for lighting effects, but often includes all 'electrical' cues, such as lighting and sound

Method acting The way of acting developed in the USA which involves actors totally immersing themselves in the part

Prompt When an actor calls for a line that he can't remember

Proscenium arch The big framing arch around the stage

Rake The sloping of some stages towards the audience to allow them to see the actors better

Stage directions Instructions in the script – either for the actors to do something, or for something to happen on stage

Stage door The door that actors use to enter the theatre, typically at the back of the building

Tab Another word for stage curtains

Wings The areas at the side of the stage, usually masked by curtains, from which actors usually enter

Index

Index

super.activ

All you need to know

0 340 773294	Acting	£3.99	☐
0 340 764686	Athletics	£3.99	☐
0 340 736305	Basketball	£3.99	☐
0 340 715189	Cartooning	£3.99	☐
0 340 736496	Chess	£3.99	☐
0 340 715200	Computers Unlimited	£3.99	☐
0 340 736275	Cricket	£3.99	☐
0 340 715219	Drawing	£3.99	☐
0 340 736313	Film-making	£3.99	☐
0 340 736291	Fishing	£3.99	☐
0 340 715138	Football	£3.99	☐
0 340 76466X	Golf	£3.99	☐
0 340 778970	Gymnastics	£3.99	☐
0 340 736321	In-line Skating	£3.99	☐
0 340 749504	Karate	£3.99	☐
0 340 715146	The Internet	£3.99	☐
0 340 736267	Memory Workout	£3.99	☐
0 340 736283	Pop Music	£3.99	☐
0 340 715170	Riding	£3.99	☐
0 340 736518	Rugby	£3.99	☐
0 340 715235	Skateboarding	£3.99	☐
0 340 736526	Snowboarding	£3.99	☐
0 340 71512X	Swimming	£3.99	☐
0 340 764465	Tennis	£3.99	☐
0 340 773332	Writing	£3.99	☐
0 340 73650X	Your Own Website	£3.99	☐

Turn the page to find out how to order these books

ORDER FORM

Books in the **super.activ** series are available at your local bookshop, or can be ordered direct from the publisher. A complete list of titles is given on the previous page. Just tick the titles you would like and complete the details below. Prices and availability are subject to change without prior notice.

Please enclose a cheque or postal order made payable to Bookpoint Ltd, and send to: Hodder Children's Books, Cash Sales Dept, Bookpoint, 39 Milton Park, Abingdon, Oxon OX14 4TD. Email address: orders@bookpoint.co.uk.

If you would prefer to pay by credit card, our call centre team would be delighted to take your order by telephone. Our direct line is 01235 400414 (lines open 9.00 am – 6.00 pm, Monday to Saturday; 24-hour message answering service). Alternatively you can send a fax on 01235 400454.

Title .... First name .... Surname ....

Address ....

....

....

Daytime tel .... Postcode......................................

If you would prefer to post a credit card order, please complete the following.

Please debit my Visa/Access/Diner's Card/American Express (delete as applicable) card number:

Signature ....Expiry Date ....

If you would NOT like to receive further information on our products, please tick ☐ .